NIGHT VISITOR!

Suddenly, Caroline wakened with a start, feeling a presence in her room. She saw the open door, remembered she had not locked it. She screamed a scream that seemed to tear her throat apart.

A man appeared, his eyes black pools of wild insanity. He leaped on the bed and caught her throat in his hands as she began to scream again.

He pressed tightly, and she felt the blood pounding in her head. His fingers were like steel—like Rudi's hands on her. But these were crushing the life from her. Her vision blurred, her head lolled back, she couldn't scream anymore. . . .

JANET
LOUISE
ROBERTS
THE
DORNSTEIN
ICON

PUBLISHED BY POCKET BOOKS NEW YORK

To Richard and Monica, Carla and Keith
Because they enjoy art, and life

THE DORNSTEIN ICON

Chapter 1

The deep purple lilac bushes were in full bloom along the avenues of Vienna. As Caroline Dudley strolled along the sidewalks, she drew deep breaths of the fragrance as greedily as she drank in the sights of one of the world's cosmopolitan cities.

"I'm in Vienna!" she murmured aloud, then grew warm with embarrassment as an older woman glanced at her in passing.

But it was indeed incredible. Her boss, Greg Alpert, had briefed her over breakfast at their opulent Victorian hotel, then kindly dismissed her to "run around all day and enjoy yourself."

He was an angel, she thought, as she had so many times since she had begun working for the art dealer three months before. She had majored in art history in college, realized that her own creative talent was minor, drifted from routine clerical jobs into store clerking. Then her parents had died in an automobile crash a year ago. Her sheltered existence had abruptly become the frantic, pressured one of a girl alone in the world.

She still shuddered as she recalled the visits to the lawyers' offices as they tried to salvage something from the wreck of her father's business. He had been an inventor, the manager of his own small electronics firm. He had given her an expensive education, her mother an elaborate house and servants, with no hint that he was deeply in debt. His death had wiped out Caroline's financially cushioned life as well as the strength on which she had depended.

She was on her own, and she was scared sometimes, scared half to death. It was so odd—to be alone. To know no one cared about her or would help her in need.

Greg was the first person she had recently met who took an interest in her. The fact that he was a handsome bachelor in his late thirties made her the envy of the girls in the women's hotel where she lived in New York. And she admitted to herself she was somewhat interested in him, and liked him more all the time.

He was never fresh—yet he noticed her clothes, and commented on a new hairdo. He was never inquisitive—yet he had made her feel like confiding in him about her drab life and the apalling loneliness she had felt since her parents' sudden deaths. He took her to dinner and taught her about wine. He escorted her to art shows and educated her taste.

"I could like him a lot, perhaps come to love him," Caroline thought, as she walked up the wide steps of the Kunst-historiches Museum, and turned to look affectionately at the statue of plump Queen Maria Theresa. She sighed a quick happy breath, then went inside. "If Greg should come to like me—quite a lot . . ."

She had noted in turning the huge man with a scar on his face. He was standing near the statue of the queen, gazing up intently, studying the motherly face of the woman who had ruled Austria so long and so faithfully. Caroline frowned as she walked up the inner staircase to the galleries. Had she seen him a few minutes before on the avenue? Or was her imagination playing tricks with her?

She forgot him quickly, becoming immersed in the magnificent paintings in the collection. She spent two hours roaming from one room to another.

It had been a marvelous day, she thought, beginning with the waking up in her red velvet bedroom. Then the breakfast with Greg, while he told her about the man they had come to see. Graf Rudolf von Dornstein was a wealthy Austrian of an old family that had suffered a great deal during World War II, when the father was murdered by the Nazis. He was an only child, the heir of the family estates and a huge castle on the marches near the border of Hungary.

"I know the icon is the von Dornstein icon," Greg had told her as his eyes flashed with the enthusiasm that only art called forth. "I am certain it is! More than all the other stolen art treasures we have uncovered—I am certain. I have never been so certain before."

"I think you have done a magnificent thing," Caroline had told him warmly. He had smiled at her, his tanned face flushed, his gray-green eyes sparkling. "Restoring all these treasures to their rightful owners, and so many years later! They must really think you are a miracle worker!"

He laughed aloud softly, pleased. "I have been called that," he admitted. "Well, it's a labor of love. I didn't ask for anything beyond what I paid for them, plus a nominal traveling fee. But sometimes the owners gave me a monetary reward, sometimes—I should say often—they became good clients of mine. Then I am able to sell them additional works by my own artists. I placed nine small paintings of Francis' last week, did I tell you? I got the letter this morning."

"Oh, how marvelous! Nine! He'll eat for a year! Have you told him?" She was pleased with Greg, happy for the enthusiastic young artist he had sponsored.

Greg grimaced. "Yes, and he threw a party that ate up half the proceeds, so I guesss I'll be loaning him money again by the time we get back!" They both laughed a little, thinking of the improvident young artists who flocked to the Alpert Gallery.

"What about the other von Dornstein items?" she asked.

"That's what I wanted to warn you about. You see, Caroline, I've never talked much to you about the way we get these lost treasures of World War II." He abruptly became more businesslike and serious. "They come to us in lots. Someone has discovered one thing, and many times several things together. Whether they are the loot of a single place in Austria, France, Germany, or Italy, we can't be certain. The drawings were discovered with the icon, and later on I acquired the statues, the little triptych, and the three paintings. I looked at them, and thought 'von Dornstein' at once. It was a hunch, I guess."

"A very educated hunch, Greg."

"Thank you, Caroline. You're a darling. But we can't be sure. I won't say I have von Dornstein items. The icon— yes. But not the others. I'm hoping the family will recognize them or have family inventories from which we can work. Or they might know another family that has lost similar things, and we can go on from there. That's why this trip might last a week, or a month. We may be just starting our search for the rightful owners."

After their breakfast conversation, Caroline had gone out to the Spanish Riding School, and watched the beautiful white mature horses and the immature gray ones practicing with their marvelous riders. She thought the Lippizaner horses were the most graceful, most beautifully trained creatures she had ever seen. As they pranced high on the sawdust to the music, the murmur of voices, the smell of sweat and horses all blended to make an indelible impression on Caroline's mind.

On leaving the Riding School she had wandered the narrow old streets, visited the apartments in the Hofburg Palace of Francis Joseph and his tragic consort, the beautiful Empress Elisabeth. She had admired the beauty of the young girl in the Winterhalter portrait, with her magnificent hair dressed long and set with huge, sparkling diamond stars. She had gone to see the crown jewels, then out again into the streets of Vienna.

Now she turned around in the painting gallery, and almost bumped into the huge scarred man. She stared full into his face, startled, angry. He was following her. He frowned down at her, his face somehow frightening her. She swallowed. This was a new kind of "gallery pest" to her. Most of them were dapper men admiring her from a distance. This huge man looked like a farmer or laborer, his huge hands as scarred as his ugly, lined face.

He turned when she turned. She looked for a guard, but none happened to be in the room. She glanced nervously at her watch, and then was appalled. She was going to be late.

She fled. Down the long wide staircase, into the hall, out the doors, down into the gardens, and across to the divided mall. She hailed a taxi as soon as she saw one, gave the directions so breathlessly that she had to repeat them twice. "Café Schubert near the Prince Hotel, please."

He finally understood, and she leaned back in the taxi

to adjust her smart white coat. Under it she had worn the
lilac wool knit and a deep purple silk scarf. They set off
her shining blonde hair and her violet eyes, at least Greg
said so. She hoped the count would approve. She sighed.
She had never met nobility. She hoped he would not be
too stuffy and formal. What did one say to a count from a
family that had a thousand-year history? She grinned a bit,
impishly, thinking it might be safer to keep her lips sealed.

She was late, as she had feared. As she left the taxi and
approached the café, she saw Greg's car out front. She
made a face, adjusted her scarf nervously, patted her hair.
Then she saw the man coming toward her, from the other
direction. He was staring at her curiously, an odd look on
his face.

She was used to men's stares, but this was different. The
man looked arrogant, rude, haughty. He was very tall, his
black curly head bare to the May breeze. His eyes were
large, black and intense, with long lashes a girl would love
to have. He wore a dark gray suit, silk, she thought, with
an immaculate white shirt and a wide forest-green tie. He
was conservative, yet fashionable. He looked restrained—
yet passionate. She wondered why she thought so, then realized it was his walk; he had a light rhythmic step like
some of the dancers she had known in New York. Like a
panther, she decided.

He kept on staring as they approached each other,
meeting at the door of the café. He opened the door for
her and bowed in an old-fashioned, courtly way. She
murmured a shy "Thank you," and went in ahead of him.

Greg Alpert was sitting in a corner, at a large round
table. He had been watching the door anxiously, and he
jumped up as soon as he saw her.

"I'm so sorry—I'm late—it was the art museum, Greg,"
she began breathlessly, then realized he was gazing past
her at the man behind her.

"Graf von Dornstein?" said Greg, and thrust out his
hand with the eager boyish smile that always made him
look younger than his years. "This is a real pleasure! I
recognized you from your pictures."

The count took his hand briefly, bowed formally, then
turned to Caroline, a strange gleam in his black eyes. She
met them, and wondered why he looked at her as though
he knew her, as though he mocked her, as though—as
though he felt contempt for her! Why contempt? She won-

dered, even as she put her fingers briefly in his, and with-
drew them again as though burned. His hand was warm,
large, strong. She didn't want to touch him for more than
a moment.

Greg had made the introductions. The man had said her
name, "Caroline Dudley," in a deep voice, with the slight
accent of an Austrian. They sat down, Caroline sinking
into a chair as her knees threatened to give way. She had
been rushing, she told herself. That was it. Rushing about
had made her tired. But she knew also it was something
about the way the man had gazed down at her that made
her feel odd.

He was so tall. She herself was tall, about five feet
seven, slightly over, and so slim she appeared taller in her
white coat. She opened it now in the warm café, and the
count jumped up to take it from her. There was a fluster
of movement, she half rose to remove the coat, saw his
glance run down over her lilac dress and purple scarf. Did
he approve? She could not tell. He gave the coat to a wait-
ress, and sat down again.

She did not need to worry about talking too much or
saying the wrong thing. Greg rushed into speech, enthusi-
astically, full of his subject. The count listened intently to
him, studying his face with his keen black eyes.

"I am practically certain it is the von Dornstein icon,"
Greg was saying, then flung out his hand, and laughed.
"No, no, I had not meant to say that! One cannot be
certain in the art world! But I want so much to believe
that it is! Would you look at it—tell me—"

"Of course I will look at it, but it will do no good," said
the count in deep tones. Greg stared at him, losing his
smile. "You see, I was only a small child when we left
Dornstein Castle and fled to Hungary. My mother took me
back to her parents, when my father was arrested by the
Nazis. I don't remember the icon, except in a very vague
way."

Greg rubbed his hand over his face nervously. "You—
but of course you would not remember—you are too
young—" he began to mutter. Caroline felt sorry for him,
his hopes dashed so soon. "But surely there is someone, a
relative, someone who has visited Dornstein . . ."

"Of course. My mother," said the count, with a slight
smile. Caroline felt abruptly furious with him. He was
playing with Greg, mocking his enthusiasm! What a mean

Chapter 2

Greg was nervous as a cat at breakfast. He had already loaded the back seat of his car, and hired a young Austrian to guard it, he said.

"God, if anything happens to those treasures, I'll go right out of my mind. Caroline, I want you to do me a favor."

"Of course, Greg. What is it?" She was eating the lightest omelette she had ever tasted, drinking coffee with so much cream in it she knew she would soon be fat. But what a way to go, she thought, with pleasure.

"Take the icon with you. It's still in my room. Pack it in your suitcase among some of you lingerie, will you?"

"Sure, Greg. Why not?"

"Thank you, doll. If that cracks or breaks, oh, God," he said gloomily. "You know, I have nightmares about that icon. It's so fragile. The paint is peeling, and I would love to restore it, but I don't dare touch it. You stick it in among your soft things, and take care of it like it was glass, okay, doll?"

She patted his large hand reassuringly and smiled at him. "Greg, nothing is going to happen to that icon," she said, in motherly fashion. "It's going to be fine. Relax."

He smiled, but he did not relax. He kept talking nervously about the von Dornstein treasures, his concern about them, whom they might belong to if the von Dornsteins did not claim them.

"There are a dozen castles around there, they could have come from any one of them. And those drawings—and that statue—you know the little one of St. Stephen? Very popular in that period. Could belong to anyone, and there are similar ones all over."

She listened, commented, tried to calm him down. He finally drank his coffee, then dashed off to finish his personal packing. By the time she had gone up to her room, he was at her door, the precious icon wrapped in a white cloth.

He walked over to the bed, reverently laid it down, and unwrapped it, layer by layer. They stood together, gazing down at the fabulous object.

It was more than one thousand years old. The dark paint glowed in its gold setting, and the face of the Madonna was so gentle and sweet yet lively in expression that it was quite distinctive. She wore a blue robe bordered in gold with a pattern that was Greek in origin. Her dark crinkled wavy hair was realistically portrayed. Her eyes were black, as black as the count's, thought Caroline, involuntarily. Her long, slim hands were pressed softly together in prayer. The painting was on wood, and only about twelve by nine inches. But so precious, so very precious—

"Like all good art, there is more to see the more one looks," said Greg, seriously. "I've just noticed the flowers in the corner. Look, did you see it before?"

"No, I didn't. Oh, Greg, it's a miniature still life. The tiny lilies in the tiny vase!"

"Exquisite." He sighed deeply. "Got to get going. I'll wrap it up, you finish packing. If I know Rudolf von Dornstein, he'll be here at exactly nine o'clock, and expect us to be ready when he snaps his fingers."

"He's used to being obeyed," said Caroline, and grimaced.

"Be nice to him, doll," said Greg unexpectedly. "He likes you, he kept looking at you. Just be your own sweet self, don't freeze up. I could help, you know."

She felt rather surprised, but agreed readily. He often asked her to be "nice" to his artists, make them feel at home in the gallery until he returned from a lunch date. Or be "nice" to a client, chat with the people until they were at ease, and he could see them. Part of the public relations job, he said.

As Greg had predicted, von Dornstein was there ringing for them at the dot of nine. The porter took Caroline's suitcase down, she carried her small cosmetic case containing the few pieces of nice jewelry she had left from her former luxurious existence. The count could not see that she was nervous inside, she thought.

"Good. On time," he said, and smiled very briefly. His dark eyes had surveyed her carefully, as though judging whether she were fit to accompany him to his castle, she thought resentfully.

Greg had already paid the bill and was out at the car. "You will ride with me," said the count. "We will lead the way. Mr. Alpert's car is loaded, even the front seat, and you will not be comfortable riding with him."

She swallowed, nervously. She did not want to be alone with the count for the two or three hour drive down through Lower Austria to Burgenland, past Neusiedler Lake, to the marches where his castle stood on a desolate hill. But Greg had said to be nice. She managed a bright artificial smile. "Fine," she said.

He took her cosmetic case from her, and put his hand under her elbow carelessly to escort her out to the car. She was not surprised to find he had a low-slung late model sports car that looked very sleek and powerful. Next to Greg's Volkswagen, small and chunky and reliable, it looked like a black panther next to a housecat, she thought, and resented it. Why should he have so much when someone else had so little?

"It is still rather cold, and will be chilly in the countryside. Do you want the top down?" said von Dornstein formally.

He obviously did not. "No thank you," she said, politely, though she enjoyed convertible-riding, with the wind blowing her hair.

They were settled. The two men conferred a few minutes about the route, then the count took his place beside Caroline in the car. "I like to drive rapidly. I hope you aren't nervous," he said.

"Not at all."

But she did get nervous, not for herself, but for Greg.

He kept losing them. The count would have to pull up beside the road and wait for the sturdy gray Volkswagen to catch up.

After the fourth such stop, the count was becoming angry. There was a frown between his eyebrows, a line at the side of his hard mouth. "Can't he drive faster?" he asked curtly.

"He could," said Caroline, tartly, forgetting her sweet role. "But he won't. Not while he has valuable art objects in the car with him. If they fall over, a statue preserved for hundreds of years could be broken in a moment of recklessness! And the paintings could be badly scratched! He would not risk it. He loves art more than anything in the world."

The graf turned to look at her, a long steady look. "The angel carries a sword in her tongue," he said, and then smiled, not pleasantly, she thought.

"I said I wasn't an angel," she said, stiffly, staring away from him at the winding ribbon of road ahead. He was very unpleasant, rude, and inconsiderate. This week was going to be miserable, she knew. If only they could reach an agreement rapidly, and then go on their way, out of his luxurious existence! Him and his jet set bride-to-be could just . . .

Unexpectedly he reached out and patted her clenched hands lightly. "Relax. Come, angel. Give me a smile, and say you aren't angry."

Amazed, she turned her head and stared at him. Sparks were still blazing in her eyes, and he laughed.

"Oh, but you are angry!" he chuckled, and sounded relaxed and cool for once, instead of cold and haughty. I'm sorry. There, do you accept my apology for your beloved employer!"

She bit her lips, fighting back angry words. He was jeering at her.

"How long have you worked for Greg Alpert?" he asked, and started the car smoothly ahead as Greg's car came up behind them once more.

"Three months," she said, stiffly.

"Only three months. How well do you know him?"

"Quite well. He is a fine person. He is very helpful to young artists, and tries hard to help them place their work. And he loves art. His greatest joy is to find these stolen treasures and restore them to their rightful owners. He has done a magnificent job," she said, warmly.

"Hum. Yes. And you, Miss Dudley, wearing an expensive knit dress which probably is two months of your salary. What is your background?"

She gasped at his rudeness, and clenched her teeth. "That is none—" she began hastily, then stopped, appalled.

"Quite. But I am curious. You are not an ordinary secretary, you know. You are very lovely, you have the bloom not only of youth, but of a luxurious existence, which is obviously not yours now. What happened? Was your father wealthy?" His tone was suddenly, unexpectedly kind.

Greg has said, be nice to him. Her hands clenched, unclenched. Finally in a stifled voice she said, "My father was an inventor. Electronics. He had his own small firm. I was raised—well. Anything I wanted—clothes, education—then—they died."

"Your parents both died? But surely they were not old?"

"It was an automobile accident."

"When?"

"A year ago," she said. And the wave of sorrow swept over her again, and she turned her face away from his to look out the side window steadily.

"And you are alone in the world?" The tone was steady, kindly, as she had not dreamed he could be.

"Yes."

"And you work as a secretary. How fortunate that you know shorthand and typing. A woman told me once she could always make a living as long as she had those skills."

She relaxed a little. "Yes, that's true. I wanted a business education, and Father encouraged me to have it, in addition to my art."

"You paint, then?"

"Only a little. I have a small talent. I can sketch, I worked for a time in the fashion department of a store," she told him, rather defiantly. "Father encouraged me to buy the clothes I liked, and some I had helped design."

"That accounts for your excellent taste," he said smoothly, and she did not know whether he was serious. "But you do aspire to become an artist?"

"No. Not like Denise Hartman."

"Denise Hartman? Who is she?"

"A friend from college. She lives in Vienna, and is working at her painting. She's going to be good, I think," she added eagerly. "She showed me some of her work last evening, and it is—oh—it is becoming good. Imaginative, unusual. She has real talent."

"Good. I should like to see her work sometime. I shall remember her name."

The conversation lapsed a little. He was driving much more slowly, she was relieved to note, and Greg had no trouble keeping up with them.

"Does Greg Alpert handle your friend?" he asked suddenly.

She jumped. She had been looking at the beautiful farmlands, the fruit trees, the lovely vistas of distant mountains and charming towns they swept through. She had been thinking what a lovely May morning it was, with the huge pansies in gardens, the lilac bushes lining the roadside, all the joyousness of spring opening before her.

"Greg—Denise? Oh, no. She is—I mean, she has pots of money," she said, rather awkwardly. "I don't think she is considering selling yet. Perhaps when she does want to, she will work with Greg. They haven't met yet, though. Denise said she wasn't ready to talk to a dealer."

"I see."

The conversation lapsed again.

They must have ridden quite a time before he spoke again. Now she did not find the silences awkward. They had broken some ice, he was not so formal and disagreeable as he had been the day before.

"Look ahead of you, no, over a little to the right as we turn," he said, finally. She looked, and spotted a castle on a lonely hilltop. "We shall be coming to Dornstein quite soon now. It is near the border with Hungary. In fact, this land over which we ride was bloodied many times with the wars between Austria and Hungary. To say nothing of the invasions of the Tatars from the east and the Turks from the south."

"Oh yes, I have been reading about it," she said, and gazed eagerly ahead of her, up toward the lonely castle, the stark stone fortress. It was like something out of a fairytale. The castle of the giant, or the ogre. Her lips twitched in an involuntary smile at her thought.

"What do you think?" he asked, his head turned toward her. "Why do you smile like that?"

Impulsively, she told him before she could hold back the words. "I think it looks like the fortress of an ogre! Out of a fairy tale!" Then she flushed violently. "I'm sorry—I didn't mean to say that—I mean—"

"Not at all. I thought the same thing as a small boy. When my grandfather lived there, and we went to see him. In fact, I called him an ogre to his face. Mother spanked me later," he said reflectively.

She burst out laughing, joyously, a little carol of laughter, and he joined her. "Oh—did you, really?" she cried. "Oh, you must have been a pair! I wish I could have seen—" Then she stopped again, very embarrassed.

"That was a very long time ago," he said, finally, sobering, and a little frown came back between his brows. They were sweeping without pause through a little village, and this time Caroline noticed that people paused to stare at him, to doff their hats, to wave, to gesture toward the large low-slung black car. He waved his hand casually toward them. "This is the village nearest to the castle," he told her. "These people worked for mine, and their ancestors worked for my ancestors, and fought with them in battles. Our pasts are as linked as our presents. My father led them during World War II, and many of them died with him."

"Oh," she whispered, and blinked back sympathetic tears as she saw an old one-legged veteran waving at them from a small cottage. She waved back at him impulsively.

Then they were sweeping up long winding road, which became progressively rougher. He had to slow down, and Greg was having trouble behind him. Caroline twisted around anxiously to watch for Greg time and again. Twice his car seemed to stall on the uphill road.

"He's all right. I am watching for him," said the count, crisply. "You need not stand guard for him!"

She whirled around indignantly, to see his amused, cold black eyes watching her expression. She bit her lips again. For a few minutes she had felt close to him. Now he had flung cold water in her face.

After a long climb, they entered a dim, quiet woods. The road was extremely rough, and even the sports car found it hard going. She knew Greg would be anxious about his paintings and statues, fearing they would topple when he hit a bad place in the road. But she said nothing, staring grimly ahead, her hands again clenched in her lap.

Then the woods opened into sunlight, and ahead was a long sweeping drive leading to the front of the fortress. It was huge and gray, of stone that looked cold in the bright sunlight. Small windows at the top overlooked all sides, so that someone could watch the enemy approaching from any angle. The count pointed out the Hungarian border, which looked quite close to her. "Ten miles away," he said briefly. "This is built on top of an extinct volcano, as many of the fortresses are."

The car pulled to a stop in front of a huge entrance way, big enough for three or four carriages, she thought. Several men jumped to attention, and came to the car to take the suitcases, coats and two rifles that the count handed to them. He himself helped Caroline from the car, then left her at once to go to Greg's car as he pulled up behind them.

"I say, your car is pulling badly," said the count. "Let's get it unloaded, and then I'll turn it over to Franz. What he knows about cars is encyclopedic. He can have it tuned up for you by the time you leave."

"Oh, this car is all right," said Greg, climbing out stiffly. "It's just your abominable road back there," and he laughed easily. "No, it's all right. I had it adjusted before I left Vienna."

"Doesn't sound right to me. Something wrong in the motor," said von Dornstein, frowning. "Franz!" He clicked his fingers commandingly. One of the uniformed men jumped forward, and the count spoke to him in rapid German. He nodded, and they began to unload the car. Greg watched them uneasily, and finally directed the unpacking, with no thought for Caroline. The count was watching them, his black eyes narrowed.

Suddenly, he turned to Caroline, who was watching the scene patiently. "I beg your pardon. Let me take you inside, and introduce you to Mother. She will see you comfortably settled." He took her arm easily, commandingly, and led her inside. The hallway was immense, lined with armor and faded battle flags, including one that looked vaguely familiar. She suddenly realized it was an American flag, only one from a hundred years ago, with fewer stars on it. She wondered what its history was.

But she forgot it at once, for a beautiful woman came out to greet them. She was tall, striking in appearance, her hair a curly raven black, and her black eyes just like Rudolf von Dornstein's.

"Mother—you are well?" Rudolf was bowing over her hand, then kissing the pink cheek held up to his. The black eyes smiled at him affectionately even as the mouth scolded.

"Two days late! Not a word from you! Bad boy!" she said in a husky musical voice.

"But look what I brought you. A pretty angel from America. Miss Caroline Dudley, Mother. Countess Theresa Mayer von Dornstein, and do not forget the Mayer, for she is a Magyar and would not have you forget her birth!" He teased his mother, and she scolded him, and laughed.

The countess escorted Caroline up to a suite of rooms on the second floor in the east wing of the fortress. The stone walls looked cold, but bright fires blazed in the bedroom and sitting room. The girl could only stare in amazement at the huge rooms, any one of which could have held her entire apartment and her neighbor's at her hotel in New York. The rooms were decorated in scarlet and gold, which added to the brightness. Several sofas and chairs were upholstered in scarlet velvet, and occasional tables shone with the patina of aged wood. Precious art objects, vases, statuettes, small boxes of ivory and silver and carved wood were scattered casually on the tables. A reading lamp beside the bed bespoke thoughtfulness. The bed itself was huge, big enough for three at least, she thought, with an old-fashioned canopy of scarlet silk over it.

"I do hope you will be comfortable here, my dear," said the countess, with a quick look around. A maid, middleaged, with graying black hair, was already unpacking one of the suitcases. "This is Trudi, your maid. She understands a little English, if you speak slowly. Trudi, this is Miss Dudley. You will take good care of her."

The maid smiled, nodded, went back to work. Caroline went over to her suitcase, and seemingly casually removed the cloth-wrapped icon, and set it aside. She knew the countess was watching her, but was too well-bred to show any curiosity. The woman soon left, saying that lunch would be ready in an hour.

Attracted by the view, Caroline went to one of the huge casement windows. She was gazing at the flat farmlands, rolling green forest lands, and the distant mountains, when her attention was attracted to a scene below her. Franz, the uniformed guard, was getting behind the wheel of Greg's car, and driving it away. She opened her eyes wide, peered out, tried to see where it was going. She thought it was away from the garage area, and back toward the road.

The car was going away. Greg's car. And the count had said the motor was defective, even though Greg had assured him it was not. Now that she thought of it, they had gone through several iron gates, and guards had unlocked them, and locked them behind the cars. She drew a deep, shaky breath. Were they afraid that burglars would get in? Probably, because there was much wealth here. Or—

Could it be that they were afraid that she and Greg would leave?

Were they locked in—or others locked out?

She shivered a little, suddenly, and Trudi quickly brought her a sweater set, from her suitcase, and indicated that she might put them on. Caroline tried to smile, and nodded her head. She indicated the gray tweed skirt that would go with them, and changed from her knit outfit into the more comfortable skirt and sweaters.

Trudi had worked quickly. The suitcases were unpacked. Caroline took the cloth-wrapped icon and put it back in one case, locked it, and indicated it was to remain on the luggage rack. The maid nodded, her face incurious. Then she beckoned to Caroline. She followed Trudi out, and down the wide formal staircase to the immense hallway below. Then the maid indicated a large room where the door was open.

"Luncheon—one-thirty," she said, tapping Caroline's watch.

"Yes, thank you."

"Come." Her hand beckoned again, she smiled a little, and Caroline again followed. The maid led the way out to the wide veranda at the front, then around the side of the fortress to one of the front wings, into a beautiful formal garden. She beamed as Caroline exclaimed in pleasure over the early roses and the huge beds of the biggest pansies she had ever seen. Trudi nodded her satisfaction, then left.

Caroline was bending over the pansies, touching an especially fine one of a purple so dark it was almost black, when she heard voices. She started, then realized they came from the drawing room beyond an open window near her.

She caught her own name, then Greg Alpert's name. It was the rich musical voice of the countess, and then the deep one of her son.

"You are sure it is Mr. Alpert, the same one?" asked the countess, in a cold tone. "Can there be a mistake?"

"No mistake, it is Gregory Alpert," said the count, in German. Caroline knew a little German, she could not catch all the words, but she found herself trembling at the coldness in their tones. "I checked his identity personally. Of course, there are others who would know—" And his voice lowered, so she could not hear.

She was staring down at the pansies, when her attention was distracted again. She gazed into the distance, frowning in puzzlement. A man, gray-haired, thin, was dancing near a fountain. Yes, unmistakably dancing, lifting his thin legs lightly in a grotesque imitation of a minuet! Caroline stared as he danced about the fountain, paused to lift a bit of water in his hand and fling it at someone, laughing as he did so.

Then abruptly he went into a rage, and cried out, swearing in German. She did not know all the words he spoke, but she caught enough to know he was protesting forcibly. "No, no, no," he was saying, and then she saw the other man come toward him slowly.

A huge man, with trunklike arms, a huge farmer or peasant, a big man with an ugly scar down one cheek, like a plow across a brown field. The man from Vienna. The man who had followed her in the painting gallery.

Caroline froze. She watched, holding her breath, not moving, as the thin old man was taken away by the huge man. He was mad, she thought, a madman dancing about, laughing, then enraged, and now babbling childishly to the huge man.

She turned and went into the house. She felt as if she were under a strange spell. A madman, and they were locked in a castle! No way to get away, now that Greg's car had been removed from him by a trick. And they had a fortune in art treasures with them, all but the jewels and some drawings that Greg had left behind in Vienna, saying he did not want to play his whole hand at once.

She was trembling. Greg met her in the huge hallway, smiling, then suddenly he saw her face. "Caroline, what's wrong?" He took one of her hands, then both of hers in his strong warm hands. He gazed down at her face in concern. "Honey—doll—what's wrong? You're cold?"

She tried to smile. "It was cold—in the garden—" she stammered, and saw the count coming toward them. "But you really must see the gardens, Greg," she said, more clearly, trying to smile. "They have the biggest pansies I've ever seen. And the most fragrant flowers—and the roses—you must see the roses—"

It was not her imagination. The count was staring at her, his eyes were cold and full of contempt, as she stood with her hands in Greg's, shaking as her employer held her reassuringly.

Chapter 3

Caroline wakened all at once, stretched luxuriously, and lay back against the plump pillows to muse. As she thought, she began to frown. Something was wrong, here at Dornstein Castle.

It was early, the sun was just beginning to stream through the lace curtains at the long French windows. She thought about the day before. Lunch had been uncomfortable, the count at his most sardonic, making jibes at Caroline and Greg in such a polite, smooth fashion they scarcely knew how to counter them. Caroline had retreated into her shell.

She had a thick shell now, one built up in self-defense. At college, and even before, she had been a shy, quiet girl, dreaming over books and art. She had been unable to act the part of the gay and vivacious belle, popular with boys. One friend had bluntly told her, a man she had somewhat admired, "You know, Caroline, you are so cold and formal, just a lady all the time! A man wants to have some fun!"

Chilled and hurt, she had withdrawn even further. She could not kiss casually, could not let a man hug her because he expected to after a dance, could not make love in cars.

She had wanted to wait for the right man. But what if she was wrong? What if the right man would not come along and find her, because he would think she was too cold and stiff to interest him? Even so, she could not force herself to be frivolous and gay and available, as some girls were.

The right man. Her mouth twisted. She was probably a fool. There were millions of men in the world and the right man could be a thousand right men—and she would not find any—or he would not find her. She sat up impatiently, swung her long legs out of the warm bed, and reached for her robe. She put it on, and padded to the immense bathroom.

In the afternoon, after the cold formal luncheon, Rudolf had disappeared. Or "Rudi" as his mother called him. Caroline's mouth curved into a little smile as she met her look in the huge mirror that covered one wall of her bathroom. Rudi. It sounded so young, like a little boy with short pants, running with a dog, racing across the gardens. The count was so sophisticated, it was hard to imagine him as a small boy called Rudi.

In any event, Rudi—or the Graf von Dornstein, which suited him much better!—had disappeared to see about something on the estate, as he had been gone two weeks, he explained curtly. The countess had shown Caroline and Greg the gardens, and some of the house.

But she had refused to talk about the art treasures. "No, no," she said, laughingly, her black eyes snapping. "My son will be angry if I let you show them to me or talk about them. He wishes me to be surprised at what you have brought. Tomorrow morning, yes? We shall meet in one of the drawing rooms, and you, Mr. Alpert, shall display the treasures to us. I can scarcely wait to see them. How terrible it was when they were all taken away!" Her vivid face had saddened, and the black eyes had deepened to a smoky hue.

And then dinner in the evening. Greg returned from going over the art treasures, looking quite satisfied. He told Caroline there was no damage done on the trip from Vienna. Nothing was scratched or chipped. "I can scarcely wait until tomorrow. But they are right. We should look at them calmly, with inventory lists at hand, rationally—oh, hell, I can't be rational about good art!" And he had flung back his head and laughed boyishly.

At dinner, Caroline had worn a long aqua dress, and her aqua-marine earrings and bracelet, left over from "before the accident." Rudi had looked at her long and thoughtfully, and seemed to approve of her. She had fastened her hair in a smooth roll behind her head, leaving her ears bare, and her long slim throat was further shown off by the low-cut dress.

"My dear, how young and lovely you are," said the countess, spontaneously, making Caroline flush. The countess seemed to say whatever came into her head, like a child. "It is good to have such youth here, isn't it, Rudi? She is like the first yellow bloom on my favorite rose bush in the garden. No—like the first flower of spring, in the woods, a little wildflower, not tame."

Caroline was quite warm with embarrassment. The count smiled at her, his mouth twisting, his black eyes dark and strange. "Do not be upset at my mother. She is poetic, like all Magyars. I should not be surprised if she composes a poem or song to your beauty. I think she does not go out in society much because she finds it too formal and stiff and cold. She would rather travel with gypsies, as we did years ago, eh, Mother?"

She smiled, and nodded, her face soft with memories. "Ah, yes, Rudi—I loved that—in spite of the worry and the danger—" She seemed to sink down into the past for a time, scarcely speaking, until she roused herself.

Greg had not spoken much, seemingly absorbed in his own thoughts. Von Dornstein had drawn him out from time to time about art and the gallery in New York, but Greg had answered only briefly, lapsing into his own thoughts. Rudolf had eyed him curiously, and Caroline had wondered at him also.

But Caroline had learned to know her employer a little, and she knew his mind was on the art treasures in his room upstairs. He was turning things over in his mind, the possible identifications, the comparisons with other art, the means of establishing possession, what price could be asked for restoring them. He was both artistic and practical, and he would be pondering over business and professional matters.

Now in the morning, with the awkward evening behind them, Caroline was also anxious to "get going" on the project. If the von Dornsteins, especially the countess, recognized the icon and some other works at once, everything would be much smoother. They could proceed at once to the less familiar items, the more difficult to identify, such as the drawings.

She bathed in the huge tub, using the bath salts lavishly, as she loved their fresh floral scent. Then she dressed in a cream suit. She regarded herself, added a cream scarf, and was ready.

She went down to breakfast, found a maid to direct her to still another dining room where the countess sat alone. She looked up, smiled, held out her hand cordially.

"My dear, we are late this morning! I am so glad you are also! Rudi and your employer have already gone off to look at inventory lists in the study, and we shall have a nice chat before we must start to work!"

"Late? Oh, dear," said Caroline, blankly, glancing at her watch. "I thought I would be early. I'm so sorry."

"Yes, I know—eight-thirty," sighed the countess. "Rudi was always up before the birds, like a little bird himself, I used to say, so curious to see what life was going to present him with that day! Such a lively little one—I can see him yet. Even today I see him with company, watching with a sparkle in his eyes to see what marvel someone is going to present to him!"

"You are like that yourself!" said Caroline impulsively. "You seem to wait—and look—with a sort of joyful expectancy to see what life is going to show you! And it may be a flower or a bird—or the marvelous lilac bushes in Vienna!"

The woman really smiled at her, a long understanding look. "And you also, my dear? Yes, of course. The way you enjoyed the lilac bushes. And are the pansies there so huge as mine?"

"Just almost as huge," said Caroline, with a soft carol of laugh that was peculiarly her own. "I adore the huge purple ones with their sweet yellow faces! And the lovely yellow ones, are so soft and pretty."

"You went to the art museums, I hope? Yes, of course. Tell me what you like best."

With this encouragement, Caroline began to chat, as she had not been able to the day before. She eagerly told of her "discoveries," the painters she had loved, how marvelous it was to see the apartments of the Empress Elisabeth. "How sad it was," she added, impetuously, "that she was so hemmed about after a youth of freedom. How she must have longed to jump on a horse and run away!"

"You understand her," the countess began when she was interrupted by a deep voice.

The count stood just inside the door, behind Caroline. She did not know how long he had been there. "It is not easy to jump on a horse and run away from responsibilities," he said, slowly, in his rather harsh way. "She knew her duty, as I hope we all do. Come Mother, I think we are ready to look at the treasures Mr. Alpert has brought. Miss Dudley? If you are ready?"

It was like a chill wind blowing through her after the warmth and real interest the countess had shown her. Caroline stood hastily, leaving the rest of the coffee in her cup. She followed the countess from the room, very much aware of the count striding close behind her.

The countess led the way to a large study. It was lined with bookshelves on three of the four sides, and a dark crimson rug covered the floor. The furniture was large, masculine, shiny with the patina of age and loving care. Behind a huge desk, Greg was setting up the statuettes he had brought on two small tables. The icon was in its white cloth, still unwrapped, but the drawings, the triptych and manuscripts and jewel cases lay opened.

Caroline was startled to see the jewelry. She had understood that Gregory was going to leave the jewels in Vienna, and show them later, when he was sure he could trust the count. Instead, he had brought them along. She glanced with seeming casualness over the display, rearranged a necklace and pendant to show off the opal against its black velvet cloth. She was puzzled, but hid it. Greg made his own decisions in his own time, and did not always confide in her. He must have had a reason for bringing the jewelry with him. Probably he had decided that evening in Vienna that he could trust von Dornstein.

She sat down in a small blue chair the count indicated. Greg finished setting up everything except the icon, which was still in its case. She saw the countess glance toward it several times. Von Dornstein seemed to have little interest in the proceedings, and was absorbed in seeing the ladies seated. He murmured to his mother about the light, was it in her eyes? Was she comfortable? Another cushion?

"Dear boy, I am fine," she said finally, settling back.

Caroline folded her hands in her lap and looked up at him wonderingly.

Greg began quietly, but Caroline knew he was very excited inside. This was the way he was at the opening of a show by one of his favorite artists.

"As you can see, these are the statuettes. I am uncertain about them. On looking at the inventory lists, I think some of them might be von Dornstein. Particularly the ones on this table," he said, and indicated the table nearest Caroline. "The small St. Stephen, with the chipped nose. The Dionysus, a distinct possibility. These four saints, quite close in identity. The small figurines, I think, are a possibility. Those on the other table were found with them, but of course Mary statues were quite common. They might be some other ownership."

He turned to the icon, and began to unwrap it slowly. Now the count was distinctly interested, leaning forward in his red velvet chair, his hawk-like face intent. The countess had opened her black eyes wide, her face was alert. The cloths were unwrapped, slowly. Then Greg turned away from them to finish the unwrapping, and said, "Caroline? Will you carry this over to the countess? Show it to her."

Caroline jumped up, surprised, but obedient. She accepted the icon with careful hands, then carried it over to the countess. She knelt naturally beside her, placed the precious wood painting in her waiting hands, and remained there while she gazed at the icon.

Caroline felt a glow come over her. The face of the Madonna was so sweetly grave, so gentle and full of expression.

"It is such a sweet face," she murmured to the countess. "I noticed that at once. Then gradually I noticed the other details, her lovely hands, and that ring. And the little flower in the darling vase." She smiled down at the icon.

"It is—it is—not the Dornstein icon," said the countess, suddenly, harshly, her melodic voice deepened. Her hands began to shake as she held the painting. "Oh, I had so hoped—but it is not. I can remember details—and it is not. Oh, Rudi . . ." And she looked up helplessly at her son.

He stood at once, came over to stand behind them. Caroline gazed up startled at them both, and it seemed the face of the count had become colder and harder. The countess' beautiful black eyes were full of tears, and her thin hands shook.

The count put his large hands on his mother's drooping shoulders. "Steady. We knew there might be a possibility it was not, Mother. You should not let yourself hope. One's hopes can always be dashed."

"But—but I had thought—it is—oh, it has to be the icon," Greg was stammering. He walked over to them, and stared down at the countess. Caroline regarded the two von Dornsteins. She felt something odd, there was a part of the scene she did not understand. Something was wrong, she felt it intuitively.

Caroline got up awkwardly. She felt as if she had been dashed by cold water. She was as bewildered as Greg. He had been so certain, and he was not often wrong. But the countess was so distressed that Caroline's first thought was for her.

"I am so sorry," said Caroline gently. "Let me put it back on the table." The icon was shaking in the thin hands. She reached down, tried to take the icon away, but the countess hung on to it for a long moment. Caroline frowned, puzzled, and finally the countess let it go. "It is too bad, but do not distress yourself, Countess. One day the true Dornstein icon may turn up, when you least expect it. Just because this one is not . . ."

"It is the von Dornstein!" cried Greg, his face flushed and angry. "I know it. I know it—I know art, and this icon is the Dornstein!"

"It—is—not," said the countess, and leaned her head against the back of the chair and wearily closed her eyes. She suddenly looked her age and older, thought Caroline, with compassion. A woman of such enthusiasm, such devotion, such love of art—this must have been a bad blow for her. Caroline carried the icon over to the table, and began wrapping it slowly and neatly into the white cloth.

"We will not say this is our final word," said the count unexpectedly. "Let us consider the matter. Yes, put it away with care, Miss Dudley. We will look at it another day, and also have experts in to see it. After all, it has been a quarter of a century since my mother last saw it. One's memory can play tricks."

"I am certain," murmured the countess. "Oh, Rudi—I had hoped—so much . . ."

He patted her shoulder. "Let us look at the other things," he said quietly.

Greg, obviously upset and shaken, began to show them the triptych, the paintings, the jewels. The countess took a more lively interest in the opals, and fingered them thoughtfully, and murmured she thought she remembered some of them. Rudi looked on in silence, sometimes consulting the inventory sheets on a small table next to him. He had resumed his seat, and Caroline sat silently nearby, watching the small drama play itself out.

It was a drama, she felt it instinctively, though how she knew she could not tell. The count was playing a part, pretending he had little interest, but she had caught the hard gleam in his black eyes. He was playing with them, a cat-and-mouse game of some kind. She felt he was contemptuous of them, by the words he used when questioning Greg about some drawing or gem.

She could not understand. They had done the von Dornsteins a great service in bringing the art objects. They could have callously sold them elsewhere, and raked in the profits. Didn't the family have any appreciation of the trouble Greg had gone to in order to collect the objects, sort them, bring them all the way to Austria? It was not as though he were asking a fortune for them.

It was a great puzzle. She sat in silence, her hands folded in her lap except when Greg asked her to show a gem or hold up a drawing. The count glanced at her when she was holding an object, otherwise, she might not have existed for him. And his mother seemed to have lost her interest in the art collection, and sat like a grieving child, brooding over the past and her memories.

Chapter 4

The art exhibition was finished long before lunch. Greg
was restless, and unhappy. He said something about "wast-
ing his time," and returning to Vienna.

"Not at all," said the count, politely. "I hope you will
stay for several days. The hunting is good, the fishing is
excellent. And Miss Dudley seems fond of wandering in
the gardens. Mother, you will want to show Miss Dudley
the greenhouses."

"I'm sorry," said Greg. "I don't wish to be rude, but I
am quite disappointed. Since you don't believe these are
von Dornstein possessions, I'd like to get back to Vienna,
and start searching for other possible owners. I believe
there are some missing objects lists there, and I want to
search them out, so the trip won't be wasted." He sounded
quite brisk and businesslike. Only Caroline seemed to realize how bitterly hurt and disappointed he was.

"I insist on your staying," said von Dornstein, smiling
rather unpleasantly. "Your car is in no shape to undertake
the return journey. I have instructed my man to work on
it until it is in excellent condition. And you must enjoy
our hospitality here for a time. It would be most rude of
me if I allowed you to leave in twenty-four hours."

Luncheon was an uncomfortable affair. Only the count seemed at ease, in high spirits for some unaccountable reason. Greg was obviously uneasy, unhappy, brooding over his plate, eating little. The countess was lost in memories of the past, occasionally murmuring something in German half to herself. Caroline sat silently on the count's right, feeling such of mixture of emotions that she could scarcely touch her food.

She knew something was very wrong. The count and his mother seemed to have rejected the entire art collection, yet his mother had been visibly moved at sight of the icon. As Caroline reconstructed the scene in the study, she thought that the countess had been excited from the first moment she had the icon in her hands. She had held it, her hands had begun to tremble, she had been unable to keep from gazing hungrily. The Madonna's face had held her rapt attention and one finger had moved to touch the little flower in the vase as Caroline had pointed it out to her.

And when Caroline had moved to take it from her, the woman had clung to it desperately. Yes, desperately. She had not wanted to relinquish it.

Yet she had denied it at once, and the count had stood behind his mother and given his support to her by placing his hands on her shoulders. Why?

At the end of the meal Greg aroused himself. "We really should pack and be on our way. Caroline, it won't take you long will it?"

She was startled but replied instantly, "Oh, yes, I can be ready quickly, Greg."

"No, no, I insist on your staying. We would be remiss in our hospitality. Mother?" Von Dornstein spoke commandingly, and his mother roused from her absorption.

"Of course, you must stay. We have friends coming— we must introduce you. And Miss Dudley, we have much to discuss, we have only just begun to be friends," and the older woman smiled so warmly and enchantingly at Caroline that she felt quite melted and helpless.

"You see? You cannot go," said the count gaily, and smiled at Caroline with some of his mother's Magyar charm. She glanced away from him, then back again. Yes, he did resemble his mother now, when the white teeth gleamed, and the black eyes sparkled, and his face was not set in stern, cold lines. She half-smiled back, then looked at Greg.

"No, we must go on, we have much to do. Thank you so much anyway," Greg was beginning.

The count waved his big hand. Caroline felt herself following its movements hypnotically. "Impossible. Your car is being worked on, and you must stay. You see?"

Gred looked angry and upset, but had to give in, though he did so with bad grace. Caroline, sympathetic, could do nothing about the situation. Greg had been hurt, and he wanted to leave. His artistic judgment had been found at fault. She could imagine how bitter he felt.

But the situation continued to puzzle her. Greg left the table, and went to the study to look at the inventory lists again, at von Dornstein's polite insistence. Caroline hesitated about following him, and was drawn back by the count's big hand on her arm. She felt its heat through the fabric of her jacket.

"Miss Caroline," he said. "You are interested in the art museums of Vienna. Let me show you some books which may intrigue you. This way."

And he led her firmly in another direction, to a large library at the end of one of the long corridors of the castle. He opened the door and she gasped at the long walls of shelves of books. They stretched on four sides, a floor to ceiling expanse broken only by a few narrow casement windows.

"This library was begun in the eleventh century," he said casually. An ancestor of mine brought back some scrolls from the Holy Land. You may be interested in seeing them. However, the art books I mentioned are on these shelves."

He opened several large manuscripts, laid some on the table, invited her to study them. She sat down rather uneasily on the tall chair he indicated, and found he was still standing over her, gazing down at the book over her shoulder. He was very close. He reached one large brown hand over her shoulder, brushing casually against her and disturbing her hair, to turn a page.

She gazed blindly at the exquisite illumination, not seeing anything at all but the large brown hand, the black hairs on it springing up as though as vibrant with life as their owner.

"Sir—graff . . ." she began awkwardly.

"Please call me Rudi, then I may call you Caroline," he said, smiling, giving her name that little accented lilt that made it sound like a special, unusual name.

She hesitated, did not name him at all. "I would like to know—why are you keeping us here? For you are keeping us here deliberately, I think," she said, with shy directness. She looked up at him, directly into the black eyes that were so difficult to meet.

It may have been a trick of the light, but his face seemed to take on a ruthless cast, his mouth seemed to stiffen.

"Of course," he said, smoothly, after a short pause. "I wish you to meet some friends. And I wish them to meet you. Some of my friends are very old ones indeed. They are familiar with the Dornstein treasures. I, as I informed you and Mr. Alpert, do not rememember the treasures at all, I was quite young. So I wish several old friends to look at the objects, and confirm my mother's opinions. I should hate for all this trouble to be in vain. It may well be that her memory is at fault. She has been through much trial, as you may well imagine."

She frowned up at him. It sounded so plausible. Yet—yet—it did not sound right. "But why keep us here if there is so little chance? And Greg wishes to return to Vienna to search inventory lists."

"Why return to Vienna? My friends are art experts. They will know more than the museum curators of Vienna. And they have seen the Dornstein paintings, the icon, the jewels, the statues. If their memories are good, they may recall some of them. And your friend will not have taken his journey in vain."

"You mean my employer," she reminded him quietly. She could no longer look into the brilliant black eyes which seemed to see through her. She gazed down at the manuscript, and he turned the pages to another illumination.

"Yes, of course. Now, I must look to his comfort, then see to some estate matters. I shall be in my study, if you wish to explore the castle further. Perhaps a little tour later in the day?" And he smilingly left her to the medieval manuscripts.

Caroline sat quietly, turning over some pages, looking at one manuscript and another. But she was not soothed by his smooth explanation, nor the loveliness of the books before her. She knew something was wrong, she knew Greg was uneasy and worried.

Presently Greg found her in the library, came in and closed the door. "Here you are, Caroline. I wonder if we can be overheard?" he asked in a low tone. He sat down across the narrow table from her. "What are you doing here?"

"The graf said I should look at medieval manuscripts," she said, a little humorously. "I think he is accustomed to ordering people about."

"I know damn well he is!" Greg burst out angrily. "The gall of the fellow." His face was flushed. "You know, my car is down at that cussed village being worked on? A dozen miles away, down a tricky road with a dozen turnoffs? I can't even get my own car! He doesn't want us to leave here, Caroline. We are practically prisoners!"

"Prisoners," she echoed faintly. The word rang an alarm bell in her mind. "Oh, Greg—"

"They are a ruthless lot, the Dornsteins! Oh, the family history is a bloody one, I can tell you. I read about them before I came. They all have wild reputations. Talk about gypsies. His mother is practically a gypsy, I heard. Raised among them, taking the law into their own hands. And his father's people were just as bad. They ruled this part of Austria for a thousand years, too far from Vienna for the law to reach them."

She bit her lips, and gazed down at the open book before her. She had found a huge folio of ancient castles, and had found Dornstein Castle as it looked in the thirteenth century. It had been portrayed dramatically by the artist. It was in the center of a thunder cloud, with lightning blazing about the towers and turrets.

"During the wars with the Turks," Greg was saying, nervously lighting a cigarette, "they locked themselves up in here, and ate their vegetables and their pigs, and finally their horses, and stayed alive for three years! Three years, God, Caroline! Imagine their nerve! The Turks finally got tired and went away. And you know what those damned Dornsteins did?"

"What?" she asked, fascinated.

"They resupplied the castle, left the women and children here with a small force. Then those damn hard-nosed warriors got more horses, and went chasing the Turks, licked them in their own tents. Then," his voice lowered, "they beheaded them all, put their heads on their pikes and burned the rest of the bodies."

"Greg!" She felt rather sick, and put her hand to her throat.

"True," he nodded, dragging nervously at his cigarette. "Read about it before I came. God. To think we are prisoners of that fellow!"

She tried to laugh a little, to ease her own horror and a scared feeling she had. "But that was hundreds of years ago! This is the twentieth century! People don't do that today!"

"They did it to Dornstein's father in a Nazi prisoner-of-war camp," he said, simply. "What do you think those concentration camps did with bodies?"

She bent her head down, and put it on her arm folded on the library table. An overwhelming wave of horror came over her. Yes, it did happen today. It could happen again. The terror, the cruelties, the unspeakable torments that man could inflict on other human beings. Man's inhumanity to man. It occurred again and again in history. No one was free from that nightmare.

She heard Greg's voice soothing her, his hand patted her head. "I'm sorry, doll. I went too far. Forgive me. I'm all worked up. God damn it, I'm so cussed disappointed! I wanted to believe those things were the Dornsteins'! Well, better luck next week, as the saying goes. We'll get to Vienna, do some searching about."

"Yes. Yes, Greg." She managed to sit up straight again. She brushed back her blonde hair. "But he is—he is going to keep us here for a time, Greg. I don't know why." She managed to keep her voice calm, but he sensed her jumpiness.

"Well, he's a bad lot. He doesn't have any respect for women, but don't worry, doll, I'll be around. Rudi von Dornstein has quite a reputation with women. He has his charm, I guess. I remember when he was a young fellow, about university age. The story is he got a young girl from a nice family mad about him, ran off with her to Italy, wrecked her reputation and deserted her. I heard it cost the family a packet of money to hush it all up. And later he fell in with the jet set. You should hear about his skiing pals. Wow. He made *Time* and *Life* magazines with his affair with that dame who left the Arab prince—remember that?"

She shook her head numbly. Greg leaned back, relaxed, told her about other stories about Rudi and his escapades. It was much the same as what Denise had told her, only more sordid. She winced again and again as Greg told her bluntly what Rudi was like. He was warning her, she thought.

The stories made Greg more cheerful, as though he reminded himself that the graf was human and made mistakes. He finally left her to go up to his room and look at more inventory lists he said the count had loaned him. Caroline found herself wondering if Rudi were keeping Greg amused with inventories as he kept her amused with his books.

She went soberly up to her own room, sat in the window seat and gazed out over the wide landscape. The castle was perched on top of an extinct volcano, the count had said, and she seemed to be able to see out for miles, over the little farms, and clumps of forest, and grazing land. She thought she saw horses in the distance. She strained her eyes, but was not sure.

Presently Trudi came to help her change for dinner. Caroline chose a blue evening gown, as the castle seemed to be a formal place. It was a blue silk, the long skirt quilted. The neck was a modest round scoop, which showed off her throat and youthful skin. She wore a pearl necklace that her father had given her on her twenty-first birthday, and matching pearl earrings. Not a jet setter, she thought, and made a face at herself in the mirror. She looked like a modest, inexperienced young woman, too small a prey for someone like Rudi—she hoped.

Greg was silent at dinner. The countess had roused to animation, and talked at length to Caroline about her youth when she had ridden wild horses without her father's permission. Something had set her remembering the days when she was young, and Caroline found her eager and charming. She could not help responding to the woman's sweetness, and answered her with memories of her own. Rudi seemed to be only half-listening, and Greg made no pretense of paying any attention. The two women carried on a quiet conversation, accompanied only by the clink of crystal and silver.

"And then my father forbade me to ride Prince again. I was furious. I adored the horse, my first black stallion. And I arose before dawn the next day, and stole out to the stables. I saddled the stallion myself, so the grooms would not be blamed. And I rode him out over the plains, all day. Oh, he was magnificent! I rode and rode, we paused only to drink at streams. I felt alive, free for the first time in my life." Her face glowed at the memory, her eyes sparkled with impishness.

"Tell Caroline, Mother, what punishment your father inflicted on you for that mischief," said Rudi in his deep voice, unexpectedly entering the conversation.

The countess chuckled. Caroline smiled in instant response. "Oh, I was punished dreadfully—Father thought! I was locked in my room. I was allowed out only to groom Prince! He was completely in my care for one week. I was forbidden to attend a party for my second cousin on his twenty-first birthday. And I gloried in it! I hated parties, I adored my horse. Father did not realize until much later he had rewarded me."

Caroline laughed out loud. "Oh—that reminds me of the time I was twenty-one and my parents had planned a party. I was so shy and miserable at parties, especially where there were dances, and I was afraid to be asked, and afraid I would not be asked. And I got sick with the measles, and it had to be canceled. My father worried about how upset I would be—and I lay in bed and read. Oh, it was wicked of me not to tell him I was happy not to have a party!"

"We must be much alike," said the countess, and launched into yet another story of her childhood.

After dinner, Greg wandered away. The countess retreated to her sitting room. Rudi invited Caroline to tour part of the castle.

"It's too large to be seen all at once, you will be only confused, Caroline. And I wish you to admire Dornstein, its strength and its beauty, as I do," he said, brazenly tucking her hand in his arm.

They were in the drawing room where coffee had been served following dinner. She felt outraged by him. Did he think he could charm her as he had charmed other women? She was another kind of woman, she thought, angrily. Not a weak pushover for his kind of man. She admired integrity and honesty. Not the kind of man he was at all.

She pulled her hand from his arm so sharply that he let her go in surprise. "I don't wish to tour your castle," she

said sharply. "I wish you would let us go! Greg and I want
to leave. Why do you play with us, in a cat and mouse
game?" She glared up at him angrily. The stories Greg had
told her about him ran through her mind, the escapades at
the university, his cruel hoaxing of the servant girl who
thought he would marry her, the forbidden duel on the
university grounds over a sixteen-year-old girl that had
caused her to be married off to a man of forty.

He regained his poise instantly, and a little smile played
about the hard mouth. "Oh, you have a temper. I had forgotten the angel carried a sword in her tongue," he said
softly. He seemed to be studying her face, especially her
mouth. She frowned at him.

"I asked you to let us go. You know that nothing is
wrong with Greg's car. I think you should get it back immediately, and let us leave! What do you hope to gain by
keeping us—pr-prisoners?" She stammered over it, but
managed to say it.

"Prisoners! You do not know what it means to be a
prisoner. I wager—no, you have not even been imprisoned
by a man's arms!" And outrageously, he caught her to
him.

She did not even struggle, she was so shocked. She
stared up at him, her eyes wider and wider, as his laughing
face came down closer to hers. His arms did indeed feel
like a prison, she thought, tight steel bars pulling her
tightly to his hard warmth.

"You see—you cannot even struggle," he said softly, his
mouth twisting with mockery. "A woman is such a fragile
thing, so soft, so easily bent and turned—and kissed . . ."
And his mocking mouth came down hard on hers in a
hard angry kiss she did not understand.

He was taunting her, telling her she could not fight either his hard arms or his charm. She tried to turn her
head away, but was held fast by his hand behind her head,
his fingers thrusting through her thick blonde hair. His
mouth on hers lost its hardness, became soft, eager,
passionate, in a way she had never felt in her life.

The kiss lasted, he lifted his head, gazed down at her,
and through blurred eyes she saw the strangeness on his
face. Then he bent his head again, and his opened mouth
clasped her open lips as she gasped for breath. They
breathed as one, her body was molded against him, bent
back against his hard arm, and his hand in her hair

moving her head back and forth slowly so his mouth could taste hers more deeply.

A storm was sweeping through her, and she felt it shaking him also. His legs seemed to quiver as he pressed himself harder to her, harder, more cruelly, until she wanted to cry out with pain, yet she longed for a more ecstatic closeness. She did not know herself. She was dizzy, shaken. Her lips moved, she was not sure if she was trying to protest—or to answer his.

Slowly, then, he began to release her, his arms loosening, his body moving back. She backed away, her hand going to her bruised mouth, staring at him with stricken eyes.

She kept on backing away from him. He was—so very strong—so very—dangerous. She backed up, and then ran out of the room. She raced up the stairs, along the corridors to her room, ran in, slammed and locked the door. She flung herself into a plush chair.

When her heart had slowed to a more regular beat, she put her face in her hands, and tried to think. She had been insane. She had—wanted—to respond. He was a dangerous man. A man of experience, she thought desperately, trying to calm her dazed mind.

He probably deserved his reputation.

He was fast and loose with women. He had dared her—and caught her up in his arms so fast—he had moved like a panther, striking her, holding her, before she knew he had taken a step toward her.

A panther—and his easy prey. She had been so easy, she thought bitterly. Her mouth still felt his hard kisses, her face still felt the scratch of his hard cheek, that dark face, pressed to hers.

Chapter 5

Caroline had great trouble calming herself. She undressed for bed, finally, though it was early. She sat for a time on the window seat, gazing out into the night sky, and across the dark Austrian landscape, over into Hungary beyond.

Finally she thought of something. Greg had given her the cloth-wrapped Dornstein icon to care for again. She had laid it on one of the small tables scattered about her huge bedroom. Now she went to it, unwrapped it with loving care, and laid it out. It had a small stand, and she set it up on the table.

She sat before it for a long time, gazing at the peaceful serenity of the Madonna's face. She felt soothed, comforted, calmed. And she was finally able to go to bed and sleep.

She wakened with a great start. She had been dreaming about Rudi, then about a great black horse that she was riding madly across hills and plains. Now she suddenly felt a presence in her room. She sat up abruptly in the huge bed, peering distractedly beyond the thick curtains of the overhanging canopy.

She pressed her hands to her breast. Oh, God, she was still having a nightmare, she thought, staring.

A tall, thin, white-haired man was crouched before the table that held the icon. His hands were curved around the wooden panel, not touching it, but gazing at it, fascinated. He was muttering words in German that she did not understand.

She screamed. She could not have kept it back. It was a high-pitched scream that seemed to tear her throat apart. She was so frightened, she knew it was the madman crouched there. She remembered him dancing about near the fountain, splashing water. And now he was in her room. She saw the opened door, remembered she had not locked it.

She screamed again. The madman had jumped up, turned to her. His face changed from calm, to a twisted demented mask. He started toward her. She screamed and screamed, the echoes ringing through her brain.

He came toward her, with his thin hands outstretched. Then someone dashed in. Greg. He flung himself at the man.

Caroline screamed again. She was hysterical with fear, as she saw Greg shaking like a rag doll in the mad grip of the white-haired man. The madman's face was a mask of hate, his eyes black pools of wild insanity. He lifted Greg up, flung him from him, dashed him down, knocking him against the wooden end of a sofa. Greg struck his head. Caroline heard the crunch, as Greg fell against it.

Then the madman turned, came toward her, light as a panther, a panther—like Rudi, she thought. She shrank back against the pile of pillows, chilled, grabbing up the covers about her. The madman leaped on the bed, crouched over her, caught her throat in his hands as she began to scream again.

He pressed tightly, and she felt the blood pounding in her head. His fingers were like steel—like Rudi's hands on her. But these were crushing the life from her. The fingers on her throat pressed relentlessly. Her vision blurred, her head lolled back.

Then the madman was pulled from her, slowly. A voice, deep, familiar, was saying soothing words. "Julius—Julius—calmly—" Then more words. Nach—Nazi—Nach —Nazi—over and over.

Finally, slowly, the fingers let up their deadly grip on

her throat. She saw through dim vision as Rudi drew the man from her. Behind him stood a huge man, the man with the scarred face, and he drew the madman away from Rudi with awkward tenderness.

Trudi stood near the door, her face anxious. As soon as Caroline was freed, the maid came over to her. Rudi brusquely told the guard to take the man away.

"Poor—poor little one," said Trudi, in English, bending over Caroline. The girl began to weep, as she caught her breath.

It had been such a horrible experience, and she could not believe yet that it was over. She clung to Trudi. Two men came in, lifted Greg, and carried him away, on Rudi's crisp orders.

Caroline could not stop crying. Rudi came over, said something in German to Trudi. The woman went away, returned with a glass.

Rudi sat down on the bed where Caroline crouched in the pillows. He brushed back her long blonde hair, gazed down into her tear-filled eyes, put his arm gently around her bare shoulders.

"I'm so sorry, little one. Little angel, it is all right now. What a frightful experience for you. Calm yourself now, it is all right now." And his hand magically soothed away her shuddering terror.

Caroline shook her head at the glass. Rudi took it from the maid. "It is just water, Caroline. Drink. Do you want a sleeping tablet?"

She kept on shaking her head. She finally managed to say huskily, "My throat—can't drink—choked."

His big hand lifted her head, turned it sideways with infinite tenderness. His fingers touched the bruised throat. "Poor angel. It is too bad. But try and drink a little, it will help. Here, I will hold the glass." And he persuaded her to try a few swallows. They did help soothe the burning sensation in her throat.

She lay back exhausted by her terror. His arm was still around her shoulders, holding her against the pillows. He was so gentle and kind she could scarcely believe he was the same harsh man who had so brutally held and kissed her. He kept brushing back her blonde hair, as though his hand loved the touch of the light silk.

A man returned, murmured to the graf, then went away again.

Rudi said, "I have been told that Mr. Alpert is recovering. I shall attend to him when you are recovered. You have both been subjected to an ordeal I would never wish to happen. Tomorrow I shall explain, and perhaps you will find it in your heart to forgive us."

She tried to say it was all right, but she was choking, and still trembling with fear. He drew up the covers about her throat, brushed his lips against her forehead, soothed her with tender words.

"Poor angel, poor little one. No, no, do not shake, you will be safe now. Be quite safe, little one. No one shall harm you." And his hand stroked her bare shoulder, her hair and her throat and her face, exerting a magic charm which did indeed help calm her.

Finally he and Trudi straightened out the covers, tucked her in gently, and Rudi left her. Trudi remained until Caroline was asleep, and came in so early in the morning that she was sitting there waiting in a chair when Caroline wakened.

The maid was very gentle and anxious about her. Caroline drank the hot tea she brought, and let her apply ointment to her throat. They covered it with a bandage, then Caroline bathed and dressed in a high-necked blue knit dress, and covered her throat with a matching blue silk scarf. Trudi brushed and brushed the shining blonde hair, and murmured lovinlgy over her.

It almost erased the bad impression of the castle of the night before. Almost. Not entirely. Caroline still felt the strong menace about her, an eerie feeling of danger she had felt since she had come to Austria.

The countess was in the breakfast room. She was gracious and charming to Caroline, examined her throat, patted her.

"How dreadful that this should happen to you here at Dornstein! I would not have it happen for the world, my dear! But Rudi shall explain. It is so terribly painful to us all—" And her lovely black eyes filled with tears.

Greg Alpert came down later, oddly light-hearted about the attack. It was as though the actual physical menace had dispelled the gloom he had felt about the rejection of his treasures. "I must be badly out of condition, since I couldn't handle the man," he said, over his black coffee. "Got to begin my exercises again when we get back to

New York. Remind me, Caroline, make an appointment for me at the gym!"

She tried to smile, relieved that he was so calm about it. She sipped her creamy coffee, swallowed painfully. She could eat only a soft-boiled egg. The bread hurt her throat.

Rudi came in as they were finishing. He looked extremely handsome this morning, she thought, as he strode in, wearing his riding habit of dark forest green. It set off his black curly hair and black eyes, his lean figure.

He invited them into his study after they finished breakfast. The countess hesitated as though she would go with them. He shook his head at her.

He said in German, very gently, "No, mama. The ordeal is too much for you. You shall not sit through all that once more. Your memories are enough. Go out in the garden, in the sunshine, and see if the gardener has planted the new rose bushes where you wanted them."

She went as obediently as a grieved child, Caroline thought, compassionately. She smiled at the countess when she turned back for a moment. The quick radiant smile lit the face of the black-haired Magyar woman, as she responded to Caroline. Rudi was watching them both keenly, a slight frown on his face, not a frown of anger, but of concentration, Caroline decided.

He led them to his study, pulled up chairs for them, sat behind his desk in a businesslike fashion. But his hands betrayed his nervousness. He fiddled with a cigarette box, lighter, a small medal set in glass which served as a paperweight.

"I did not want Mother to remain," he began finally. "All this brings back such sad memories that she would brood for days. And she is melancholy enough. I cannot get her to return to Vienna, or to see some of the old friends who fought with the Nazis instead of against them. I cannot persuade her that much of Austria was bitterly divided, that it was difficult to make these decisions. Not many fought against the state, you see."

"Many did," said Greg, unexpectedly, stretching out his long legs. He seemed much more relaxed this morning. "Your father fought them gallantly, so did many other Austrians, who were intelligent enough to know that Hitler's way could lead only to destruction."

Rudi seemed rather startled, studied him with keen

black eyes, finally nodded. "You are good to say so," he said. "My father was always a rebel. And he thought for himself. The villagers followed him devotedly, so he had a strong force—for a time. Well, that is what I wanted to tell you. My mother's brother, younger than she, gallant, a young romantic university student was—is—Julius Mayer. He joined the underground, was a liaison man with my father for a time. But they were betrayed, my father, my uncle, many others. They were caught. Tortured."

"Oh," whispered Caroline, her eyes wide, following every change of expression on his face. He did not look up at her, he was staring now at the paperweight he held in his hands, turning it solwly this way and that, gazing at the medal inside. "And they lived."

"My father was tortured, but would not talk. He was executed. My uncle was forced to witness all that he went through. He did not talk either, Uncle Julius. He went mad, completely insane. You saw the results last night."

"Uncle Julius—that was your uncle last night? The madman?" asked Greg when Caroline could not speak.

Rudi nodded. "He had adored my father, looked up to him. When he went insane, he was tormented by the delusion that he might have betrayed him to the Nazis. He babbled on, during the years in concentration camps. In brief moments of sanity, he showed such courage and fearlessness that he drew men toward him. Men like Kurt, his guard. Kurt was captured later, tortured, disfigured. You have seen his face. It was done to him deliberately. Julius rescued him twice, with such daring and imagination that Kurt became devoted to him. When the war was finally over, Kurt came to Dornstein with Uncle Julius. They have remained here with us."

"And you—during the war—" Caroline finally murmured, when he had been silent for a time.

He stirred, looked up at her briefly. His eyes were clouded with sad memories. "My mother got herself and me away, to some Hungarian relatives of hers. We traveled with them as gypsies for a time. We roamed over the Balkans for years." His mouth twisted with humor. "I'm afraid, that as a small boy, those were happy adventurous years, years that I never forgot. I did not know the danger we were in, though we played games in which I learned to evade our enemies. I had my own horse to ride, and we lived in the mountains and in caves. I loved it."

Caroline smiled with quick sympathy, stirred by the thought of a small black-haired boy playing at danger in the mountains, loving the wild, free life.

He was studying her face, curiously, and his gaze lingered on her mouth. Greg interrupted the thoughts she began to have of the way he had kissed her the night before, of his tenderness when she was hysterical with fear.

"And did you know your father had been murdered?" he asked.

"Not until we returned to Austria. When the war was over, we finally heard the news, and returned. My God, the horror of it. Mother finally broke down. She retreated to Dornstein, gradually became reconciled to the reality of what had happened. But she would find out that someone had been a Nazi, or in the Austrian army, and would turn from him with such horror and reproach, that I scarcely dared invite anyone here without a thorough screening first. I lived with her, cared for her. Uncle Julius was a trial at first, remembering no one. He now seems to remember me and mother. I was finally able to go to the university, but I returned frequently to see to the estate. Mother's happiest times are when we are able to visit our Hungarian relatives, but as you know with their Communist regime that is often very difficult."

Once Rudi had told them the facts, and seen their sympathetic interest, he seemed to relax. He leaned back, and talked more freely about the war years. He went on finally to the history of Dornstein castle.

"It has been a major castle for many centuries," he told them, with pride. "As it is in such a strategic location, it has seen the tides of war sweep up and back again. The Tartars, the Mongols, the forces from east, west, south, north, finally the terrors of the Turkish invasions—Dornstein has witnessed them all, and lived through them."

"You are right to be proud of Dornstein. I should like so much to look out of those little windows at the top, the way the defenders did—" Caroline stopped abruptly, blushing at her daring and her romantic fantasy. "I mean, I would like to see it if you have time to show me."

He smiled at her, with such heart-stopping charm that she wanted to look away and could not. "I shall enjoy showing you the castle, and those little windows. As a boy, I used to play up there in the towers, pretending I was defending Dornstein against the Turks. I vowed then I would always protect Dornstein, and all my people, with the last drop of blood in my body." His smile was gone abruptly, he was grimly serious. "Who attacks us, attacks me directly. I have so vowed it."

He seemed to be watching her face carefully, glancing now and then at Greg as he talked more of the history of the castle. Greg asked him about the Turkish invasion, the storming of the castle for three years.

Rudi laughed out loud. "Oh, that story! Everything gets so exaggerated. Three years? No, it was a winter siege. About seven months, which was bad enough. They finally gave up, those Turks. They got restless, and drifted away, and the Dornsteins and their people were able to go out into the fields, and plant crops once more."

"Didn't they follow the Turks and attack them?" asked Caroline rather timidly.

He frowned a little. "Well, one of the Turks had captured a hostage, the younger brother of the graf. He was tortured and killed in sight of the castle, to make them surrender. No one surrendered. But my ancestor did follow the Turks to their camps. He captured the man who had killed his brother and did the same to him. Then he put his head on a pike and displayed it as a warning to all who might be tempted to attack a Dornstein. This was many hundreds of years ago," he added, with a little laugh, to relieve the tension.

Caroline was shuddering a little. The story had been exaggerated, but it was true in part. Enough to make her feel abruptly uneasy again about being the virtual prisoner of the man descended from such relentless men. How would Rudi have acted, if he could have gotten his hands on someone who had caught and tortured his father?

His eyes regarded her thoughtfully, seeming to study her. Again Greg interrupted their thoughts. "I was wondering about your family motto. I thought it would be something like, 'Death before Dishonor,' or 'Austria, Dornstein and family,' or something similar," he said, in a half-joking vein.

"No, it is the old Latin tag, 'Ad Astra Per Aspera'," said Rudi, quietly, his voice taking on a strong ring of steel. "Through difficulties to the stars. You know it, Caroline?"

She nodded her head. He seemed to be saying something significant, just to her. All their conversation seemed to be filled with significant double meanings, and she could not figure out anything. Now he seemed to be watching them for their reactions. He would say something, then watch guardedly for how they responded to him.

She sighed. She was tired of mysteries, and her throat ached. All this talk of the past had upset everyone, she thought. Rudi was bitter at the memories, his mother deeply hurt, she was saddened. Even Greg seemed more thoughtful, though he seemed more self-assured today, after his crushing disappointment of the day before.

"We have talked long enough of sad things," said Rudi, and pushed back his tall chair abruptly and stood up. "Come, Caroline, let me take you to Mother in the garden, and let her show you the flowers of which she is so proud. You must admire her roses, or she will be truly disappointed."

"I shall not disappoint her, I think the flower gardens are the most gorgeous I have ever seen," she said, lightly.

Greg said, "I'm going up to study the list some more. You say some of the experts will be arriving in a day or so? I hope someone will recognize some items."

"You may be sure they know Austrian art," Rudi reassured him, but there was that ring of steel in his voice again. He took Caroline's arm in his hand and directed her out to the corridor, to the huge front doors, and out into the gardens. He still held her arm, as though he had forgotten he held it, or as though he had a right to hold her, she thought, rather resentfully. "Ah, here is Mother. Where is the yellow rose you wanted to show her?" And he turned Caroline over smoothly to his mother, and left them.

Chapter 6

That afternoon, the guests began to arrive. Dinner that evening was much more formal and lavish. Caroline sat quietly in her place farther down the table from Rudi. The place at his right was taken by a formidable woman who seemed to be held in much affection by Rudi and his mother.

Caroline guessed Madame Gerda Zollner was a dowager of about seventy. She wore a rustling black dress, and her white hair was piled high and crowned by a small but excellent tiara. She talked constantly, listened little, probably because she was deaf and because what she had to say mattered more to her than what people said to her. Rudi smiled at her, patted her hand, listened to her with flattering attention, winking (outrageously) at Caroline a couple times.

But Madame Zollner did know art. Greg Alpert, inclined to be contemptuous at first, was leaning across the table, straining to hear her opinions on past and present art.

"Oh, yes, I remember that collection well," she said, when she finally caught his eager question. "Studied it, helped with the catalogue. Yes, yes. Several dubious pieces in it, though. Did you know it was finally decided that the Raphael was of the school of Raphael, not by the master? Had most of them fooled for a time, but I caught some touches, the brush strokes, you know. My eyes were always excellent."

"Still are," said Rudi, patting her hand. "I am counting on you to tell us if the icon is the real thing."

Greg visibly stiffened, his eyes lighting with excitement.

"Well, I shall. When shall we see it?" asked Madame Zollner, imperiously. "I am anxious to see all the treasures Mr. Alpert has brought. One family has especially commissioned me to watch for some of their missing statuettes."

"Good, good, I know Mr. Alpert will be pleased and relieved. He has wanted to return to Vienna to consult the museums. I told him my group of friends could identify items much more accurately, you are all experts," Rudi was drawling. "Frieda and Erich Bosse arrive tomorrow."

His mother frowned at once. Madame Zollner said bluntly, "Those Nazis! I wonder that you will allow them within a hundred miles, Rudi! I have told you—"

"Yes, yes, my dearest! But they know jewelry, and Mr. Alpert has brought some pieces amazingly like those of the Dornsteins."

Caroline glanced eagerly toward Greg, was amazed to find him pale, staring at Rudi. He began biting his lip nervously. Did it upset him to think of Nazis? She knew he felt bitterly about World War II, his brother had been injured badly in western Germany. All the old hates lingered, she thought.

Wolfgang Gruber, an elderly man seated across from Caroline, leaned forward. He was frail, white-haired, with a gentle, absent expression. He said, "But those Nazis, really, Rudi, is it necessary? They will only upset your dear mother."

Rudi looked at his mother, a long, speaking, significant look. The countess returned his gaze steadily.

"The war is over, long ago," he said finally. "Mother has agreed that Frieda and Erich come, also, of course, Irma and Bruno Hinteregger. They know the drawings quite well, having seen them as they were confiscated."

The countess muttered something. Her words were drowned as Madame Zollner tapped Rudi's big hand playfully. "And the Hintereggers' daughter, the lovely

Winifred? She comes also, yes? Ah, ha! I sensed the ro-
mance! Your names are in those gazettes, and she wearing
those ski pants. Is she as lovely as ever? Blonde and
green-eyed? Like a painting by one of our best German
artists?"

"As lovely as ever," he agreed smoothly. Caroline was
watching his eyes, the black eyes so enigmatic, and he
glanced at her and found her watching him. Again he
turned serious, studying her, and she looked down at her
plate uneasily.

Madame Zollner piped up again, this time embarrassingly. "And is the lovely Winifred as beautiful as this
young American girl here, with her pretty pink and white
skin, and her violet eyes, and her long legs? Hum? Or is
this young lady more beautiful?"

Caroline blushed violently. Wolfgang Gruber stared at
her, nodded, and muttered a compliment in German. The
countess reached over to pat her hand.

Rudi said, "They are each beautiful, in their own ways.
Miss Dudley is like an angel, yes? And Winifred—well,
she is not an angel," and he laughed.

Caroline bit her lips, and wished she dared say something sarcastic. How could he be so rude? The countess
said, "You are embarrassing her. How can you speak so
personally, Rudi?" she rebuked him mildly. "I love this
dear American girl because she admires my flowers, and
loves to hear me ramble on about my long-lost childhood.
We have a rapport, yes, my dear?" She smiled kindly at
Caroline.

Caroline murmured, "Thank you," but her hand was
shaking when she lifted her wine glass. She sipped a little at
the white wine, shook her head when offered more by the
prompt footman. She was intensely aware of Rudi studying her. She wished he would look away. When Winifred
came, she could have all his attention, and welcome to it!

The evening was spent in the countess' drawing room.
Coffee was served, and the conversation turned readily to
the past. All the guests had been often at Dornstein in
"the old days," when Rudi's father was alive, when Julius
was a gay young blade at the university, when Rudi was a
baby. Caroline sat in silence, immeasurably saddened by
the wistfulness of their reminiscences of days which would
never return, of people whose lives had been so cruelly cut
short.

The next day was much worse. Baron Hans von Ehrenberg arrived, an excitable, gray-haired man in his fifties, with green eyes and a strong temper. He had been helped by Gregory Alpert years ago, in the restoration of some of the Ehrenberg treasures, and was embarrassingly grateful to him.

Greg was unmistakably startled to see him, and retreated into his shell of brisk businessman. He told Caroline later, "God, I was stunned. You know, he broke down and cried when his things came back. Most embarrassing scene I ever saw. I think he is mentally unstable."

"I wonder that any of them are, after all they have gone through," she said, softly.

Frieda and Erich Bosse arrived in mid-morning. Only Rudi greeted them calmly. Wolfgang Gruber and the Countess von Dornstein were unmistakably hostile. The others retained a coldness, which made Caroline realize anew how the old hatreds lingered.

They had been Nazi collaborators, Greg had told her. He knew their record. Her mother had been held prisoner by the German Nazis, so the Bosse family had told secrets, betrayed some of their fellow Austrians, helped steal jewels from noble estates, only to find at the end of the war that her mother had been killed soon after her imprisonment. An old and sordid story, often repeated.

Caroline watched the aged, bitter faces of the couple, and thought, "How much they must regret. Were they weak, or were they simply so devoted they would do anything to rescue her mother? How complicated motives must be in a war."

How would Rudi have reacted if he had been an adult at that time? He would have done exactly as his father had, fought with any weapon at hand to defend his own, and his honor. He was that way. She wondered why she could be so sure. He was a charming man and had a reputation with women, but she also felt completely sure that when the chips were down, he would fight to the death to defend his own.

Before lunch, the last of the guests arrived. The most important were Irma and Bruno Hinteregger, and their beautiful daughter Winifred.

Caroline was amazed by her. She had never seen, even on the New York streets, a woman so assured, so like a model in the perfection of her makeup, her clothes, her hair, her style. She was something from a glossy magazine, staged and unreal and poised. Yet, a woman. She betrayed it when she turned to Rudi, slipped her tanned hand in his, matched her long stride to his, and leaned against him as they walked to the door of the castle.

She laughed, an intimate, assured laugh. She gazed up at him, and her green eyes betrayed her longing. When she was introduced to Caroline, she glared, and her catlike eyes narrowed. She was jealous at once, and Caroline told herself she was flattered.

"Do you ski?" was one of her first questions.

Caroline answered with simplicity. "No, I work," And was surprised when Rudi burst out laughing. She glanced at him, her eyebrows raised.

"You are crushed, Winifred, my darling," he said caressingly. "This little angel works. You do not, you play. But you are lovely, anyway, even though you are so useless!"

She pretended to strike him with a tanned fist, laughing.

"Many working girls ski, you know," Winifred said patronizingly to Caroline. "You could learn. I suppose you have some physical coordination?"

"I suppose I could learn. I don't have the time or the money to do so, however," she said, quietly. She thought Winifred would lose interest, but the girl was persistent, asking her questions all through lunch.

The questions and Caroline's answers revealed all too clearly the worlds apart they were. Winifred asked about night life in New York.

Caroline's face lit up. "Oh, I often go to the opera and the ballet, they are so wonderful there. I saw the Stuttgart Ballet recently, you in Europe can be very proud of them."

"Ballet!" and Winifred flung up her hands. "Opera! Oh, you are impossible! I mean discoteques! Don't you dance?"

"Only ballroom dancing, I'm afraid." Rudi was listening with cool amusement to their exchange. Greg was frowning over his own thoughts. The countess listened intently to each of them, turning thoughtfully from one to the other, the two blonde girls so tall and slim, yet so different. One so tan and sophisticated, one so pretty and unaffected.

The other guests were proficient in their fields. One

knew drawings and prints. One was an expert on paintings. One was famous for his knowledge of iconography. Greg listened to their talk, respectfully, withdrawing into his shell.

After luncheon, Caroline and Greg spoke to Rudi, on Greg's urgent request. He met them in his study.

"Yes, Mr. Alpert? You wished to ask. . . ?" Rudi offered cigars, which Greg refused.

"I say, I had no idea you could commandeer such a group of art experts," said Greg, eagerly. His hands were fidgeting with his lighter as he played with a cigarette. "I want to return to Vienna, gather up several more items I left there with a friend."

"I thought you had brought everything with you as I requested," said Rudi, smoothly, a slight frown between his eyebrows.

"Only those items I thought might possibly be Dornstein," said Greg, with a brisk professionalism that Caroline knew masked some uneasiness. "I have some more items there I had hoped to find out about through the museums. I want to go back, get them and come back. Lord, I couldn't hope to get such a group together if I stayed a year!" And he laughed, with a false ring which made Caroline wince.

"There is no hurry. Franz tells me your car has some serious difficulties and will take several more days to fix. He is a perfectionist, and I should warn you it will take almost a week to bring the car to the peak of perfection which Franz demands."

"Oh, Lord, I don't care about that," said Greg brushing his hand in the air vaguely. "Just so it gets me to Vienna and back."

"And Miss Dudley? You don't care about her safety on our mountain roads?" The smile was edged.

"Oh, I have ridden with Greg hundreds of miles," Caroline said, but neither man was paying attention to her. She had the positive feeling that they were sparring with each other, testing each other, and she was not involved at all, nor part of their argument.

"She can stay here and enjoy the guests," said Greg. "While I am gone, if she feels like it, she could start working on the art collection with your guests. She knows almost as much about it as I do!"

"Indeed? I did not get that impression. I thought she

was not long out of school," said Rudi, politely, but with the deadly edge in his voice that was just short of rudeness. "I thought the collection was of your own gathering. Hasn't Miss Dudley worked for you only three months?"

"Oh, but—yes, of course, but she knows art, and she can just show the drawings to those experts—and the icon—and all that," Greg tried to laugh. His cigarette was still unlighted. Rudi picked up a lighter and held it out for him.

"No, no, they are your find. You must get the credit. And they will need to question you about where the drawings appeared, and the statuettes, and the other objects. You know, the Bosses are employed by the state to help identify some of Austria's lost art treasures. It is part of their work to come here, and not only identify the objects but also trace who had them. Some persons who stole the treasures during, and some who received them in the United States later are still loose and unpunished. It is our duty not only to recover the art, but also to punish the criminals," said Rudi casually.

"I don't see how that can be done after all these years," said Caroline. "It has been more than twenty-five years. How can they possibly trace all those objects through the various hands that held them? And some of those receiving the goods must surely be innocent of any wrongdoing."

"That is all beside the point," said Greg, impatiently. "Look, von Dornstein, I want to return to Vienna. I have some business there, besides picking up the rest of the art treasures. I can be back in three days, just let me have the car and be on my way. The sooner I go, the sooner I come back."

"I could not consider it," said Rudi, very politely, very coldly. "My guests are here to see you and talk business. You must remain. Also Miss Dudley. Excuse me, I must talk to my steward now. Tomorrow we will get to work in earnest. I suggest you might wish to spend the afternoon going over the records of the treasures, to try to recall where each appeared."

And he left them. Greg muttered angrily, excused himself to Caroline, and returned to his room. Caroline felt uneasy. Greg was obviously anxious to leave, Rudi determined he should not leave. What was going on?

Before dinner, they gathered for cocktails in the drawing room. Caroline refused the alcoholic drinks, so did the countess. But Winifred wandered about, glass in hand, and needled Caroline, to whom she seemed to have taken a dislike. Greg was buttonholed by Baron von Ehrenberg, who became more insistent on expressing his gratitude in tearful terms the more he drank.

"No, no, you must let me tell you," said the baron, following Greg as the red-faced man tried to move away from him into the crowd. "If it had not been for you, the Ehrenberg diamonds would be lost forever! I am convinced they were going to rip them out of the necklace and tiara, cut them into smaller diamonds, and sell them on the market in South America. We should never have traced them, once they were cut!"

"I was glad to find them, glad they turned out to be genuine," said Greg, curtly. He frowned down at his scotch and water. "It is always satisfying when one's artistic judgment proves accurate. You enjoyed seeing the drawings and paintings again, I think? Good. They were really what led me to the diamonds. Just a hunch."

"An educated—hunch, as you say," said the baron, tears in his green eyes. "Ah, when I think how pleased my dear mother was, before she died, to hold the Raphael in her hands once more, that small exquisite painting she remembered so well. . ."

"Yes, yes," said Greg, trying to edge away. The baron followed, persistent as a mosquito, saying yet again how grateful he was.

Winifred Hinteregger had been standing beside Caroline listening. Now she said, her lovely mouth smiling, her green eyes cold, "How much satisfaction some people find in work! As though it were a god! Don't you agree?"

"Some people find much satisfaction in work," said Caroline, quietly. "I do myself."

"Would you work if you had money, as much money as you wished?" asked Winifred, her mouth curling unpleasantly. She spoiled her effect, thought Caroline. She no longer looked like something out of a glossy magazine, smiling pleasantly from behind her goggles on a dazzling white ski slope.

"Yes, I would."

"How do you know?" Winifred persisted. "How can you tell? I'll bet you any amount of money you would laze about, skiing and running about as I do. What is the good of working? You only take work from someone else."

"But Miss Dudley worked even when she was wealthy," said a deep voice behind Caroline. Startled, she turned to find Rudi. Listening again, she thought, with resentment.

"Oh, were you rich?" asked Winifred, looking down at Caroline's simple pink cocktail dress and single strand of pearls. Her fingers, covered with ruby and emerald rings, flicked nervously at Caroline's single-drop earrings. "That doesn't look it. Did you have to sell everything?"

The girl was crude, thought Caroline. She looked around the room without answering.

"You didn't answer my question," said Winifred, smiling. "I asked . . ."

"I don't have to answer personal questions," said Caroline, mildly. "Excuse me." And she walked away, leaving Winifred laughing behind her.

The countess beckoned urgently to Caroline. Caroline hesitated, then gave in to the charming smile, and went to Rudi's mother. The countess patted the couch beside her, and Caroline sank down gratefully. Sanctuary, she thought. The countess didn't like Winifred Hinteregger either, because of the Nazi background of her father.

"My dear, do tell the baron about your experiences in New York. I have been trying to persuade him to travel, he is young yet. He ought to go to New York. Wouldn't he adore the ballet and the theater? Do tell him for me." And the countess took Caroline's hand and held it, as though to comfort her. She knew, thought Caroline. She knew that jet set heiress had been needling her.

Caroline talked to the baron slowly, pronouncing the words carefully as his English was not very good.

Raised voices in one corner made them all turn quickly.

"Oh, dear," said the countess, and muttered something in German. "Oh, those pigs," she said, which Caroline had no trouble in translating.

Frieda and Erich Bosse were evidently in an argument with Madame Zollner. The deaf woman was flushed and agitated, her back stiff and straight in her old-fashioned black dress. Her head quivered with indignation.

"But to betray your friends, and again and again, to see their precious works taken from them, how could you? It is the same story. One thinks more of his precious skin than of honor! Life is more than integrity. I cannot bear the whining excuses of those who would cover up their notorious activities . . ."

Rudi had made his way rapidly to their corner. He soothed, cajoled, pleaded, spoke humorously. Finally Madame Zollner's voice lowered, and her flush died down. The Bosses turned and made their way over to the Hintereggers. Caroline felt the countess sag with relief, and give a little sigh.

"So difficult," she said with a smile to the baron. "That's why I told Rudi I didn't want them here! It always makes trouble, and I do dislike trouble. Quarreling and arguing about the past, it does no good, correct? I would rather quarrel with a weed, or argue over a flower."

"But my dearest countess, you have made your peace with the world," said the baron, thoughtfully. "Your gracious spirit has found reality in a rose, precious treasure in a pansy, loveliness in lilacs. May I take lessons in acceptance from you? I should try to be a good pupil!"

And from the way he looked at the lovely lady, Caroline knew at once, that he loved her, that he respected and admired her as everyone seemed to.

"What a sweet speech, and in English too," said the countess, with a pleased little ripple of laughter. "Was that not prettily done, Caroline? Tell me, what is your philosophy of life, my lovely American friend? You too seem to have tranquility of spirit, and at so much younger an age than I!"

"Oh, I don't know if I have it. I just try to accept things as they are, and be happy," said Caroline, rather startled at the compliment. "When one has work to do that one likes, and friends, it makes up for—for most things." She thought of the way her parents had died, how hard that had been to accept, and a little tremble came into her voice.

"And besides, she is an angel," came the deep voice behind her, and once again she turned to find Rudi behind her. He laughed down at her. "Angels are always sweet, are they not?"

She blushed violently. She had been feeling so peaceful with the countess and the baron. Now Rudi was here, disturbing her again. "I wouldn't know," she said, with hostility, her violet eyes flashing. "I am not an angel, I told you that! And I don't know any angels!"

"I do," said Rudi, and turned away at Winifred's tug on

his arm. She drew him away to the curtained French windows, and presently they were out on the balcony. Caroline tried not to mind that they had left the room, nor to wonder what they were doing out there in the fragrant spring evening.

It was none of her business. She was here to work with Greg. What happened to these people, the Dornsteins and their friends, was none of her business—and she did not, did not care! she told herself passionately. Yet she felt somehow it was untrue. Her life seemed interwoven with theirs, already, with their wild rebellious thousand-year-history, with their castle, with their loyalties, and with their hates and passions.

Chapter 7

Caroline was glad to leave the company and go to bed. She locked her door firmly in spite of Trudi's earnest assurances.

"But indeed, Miss, the man is locked in his rooms, he will not come! You are quite safe in Dornstein! And what if there should be a fire? No, no, do not lock the door."

Caroline just smiled, pushed her out firmly and locked the door. She would not take any more chances. She rubbed more ointment on her throat. It hurt tonight, she had strained it talking and damaged it further, she thought. She got into bed and was irritated by the fact that she was unable to go to sleep immediately. She was tired.

But she kept thinking of Rudi, with Winifred's possessive hand on his arm. The way he looked down at her, amused, interested, his eyes intent on her beautiful face. Did he love her? Would he marry her when he had persuaded his mother to the match? Probably. They deserved each other, she thought, spitefully. Then she wondered. Would Winifred live up to the code of the Dornsteins? Did she have the honor, the integrity, the loyalty the family demanded? Caroline was not at all sure. It would be a pity, she finally decided, tossing restlessly in the large bed.

The countess would probably never like Winifred. And the jet setter would fill Dornstein with noisy friends, dance to popular records in the charming ballroom, race in a fast car to the nearest ski resorts, neglect Dornstein . . .

"Oh, what does it matter to you?" Caroline muttered, and was appalled to find it mattered a great deal.

"You love him," she whispered finally against the pillow. She winced. She did not want to love someone like Rudi von Dornstein. He was from another world, a world she would be glad to leave. A world of thousand-year hates, deep passions, wealth she did not dream of, jewels and paintings and a dozen gardeners to keep the roses beautiful. And madness and ancient loyalties, and heads on pikes, and disfigurement in concentration camps.

She shivered. She did not want to love. Yet love had come unbidden. In the caressing touch of a man's hand on her throat, the sudden hot passion of his lips against her open mouth, the gentleness of his voice as he soothed her terror, the scratchy feel of his cheek against her smooth skin. "I love him—I don't want to love him—but I love him—" she whispered to the darkness, staring out at the dim light of the casement windows.

"Oh, I never thought love would be like this, so painful, so distressing. I don't want to love! But—to feel his arms about me—and when he went with Winifred to the gardens—I felt pain, and hate, an ache as though he had struck me."

She finally slept, to dream of Rudi, of walking with him in a peaceful garden, hand in hand, until he turned to her and held her in his arms. She wakened, smiling, remembering the touch of his warm lips—to find herself alone in bed, with the sunlight caressing her face.

"Oh, I'm a fool!" she told herself, and jumped out of bed, blushing at the thoughts she had had the night before. But she put on the lilac wool suit because he seemed to like her in lilac, and she wore a scarf to hide her bruised throat. And Trudi brushed her hair into a long shining length, not upswept, because he seemed to like it better long.

She had never dressed for a man like this in her life. Looking at herself anxiously in the mirror, to see if there were anything she could improve—trying to see herself as he would—wondering what he thought, worrying—anxious to be just right.

She went down to breakfast, and was horrified at how disappointed she was that he had breakfasted early and was out on the estate. She would be leaving in a few days, she told herself sternly, and never would see him again. This was ridiculous, to feel pain at not seeing a man she had not known existed a few days before.

She forgot her feelings immediately when Greg murmured to her that they were all going to meet in the large library after breakfast and look at the treasures. "And they are all art experts. God, I hope they can figure things out!"

He was so nervous that she patted his hand. "I'm sure they will be able to help identify everything, Greg. Just think, how marvelous to be able to restore all the art to the rightful owners."

"Right. And the contacts are invaluable. I may get some more stuff back in the States, and bring it back to them." But he still seemed nervous and upset, jittery over his precious treasures. He scarcely touched his breakfast, but hurried off to arrange the material.

She soon excused herself and followed him. She went to her room to get the icon, and brought it down to the library. Greg was already busy setting out the drawings, the statuettes, the jewelry. Caroline set up the triptych, helped with the jewelry. The guests began to trickle in, trying to restrain their eagerness as they walked from one display to another.

Finally Rudi arrived. The countess did not appear, but all the other guests came, even Winifred, watching all with polite amusement.

"Um, um," said the baron, and leaned down to peer at the pile of prints. He lifted one after another thoughtfully, and inspected them with his single eye-piece.

"Ah, the icon! I remember it well!" cried out the quavering voice of Wolfgang Gruber. He half-knelt beside the table on which Caroline had stood the icon. "Ah, that lovely gem! The precious face of the Madonna, I remember every detail! The icon has returned!"

Rudi went quickly to him. "Do not say so quickly that you identify it, Herr Gruber," he said, rather sternly. "You will raise hopes that might be dashed. Please exam-

ine it at your leisure. Do you wish a glass for inspection?"
And he handed him a magnifying glass.

Herr Gruber looked at him, then at the icon, and began
to simmer down, Caroline thought. He accepted the glass
meekly, and sat down to inspect the object carefully. The
baron peered over his shoulder, his mouth worked for a
moment, then he returned reluctantly to the prints. The
Bosses were already examining the jewelry. Others took up
the statuettes, turned them, examined the wood or marble
for cracks. They did not consult the inventory lists scattered about by Rudi and Greg. There did not seem to be a
need for that kind of checking.

Greg became more and more silent and withdrawn. His
face became pale and anxious as the guests silently studied
the objects. He answered only briefly any questions put to
him, as to where the drawings had turned up, where the
icon was found.

"I am sorry. It was brought to me, through contacts.
They knew I did not ask many questions. I was anxious only
to restore the art to the rightful owners. No, I am sorry. I
did not ask, deliberately. That has always been my policy. I
have been able to get many lost objects that way."

Stubbornly, he clung to his policy. Caroline began to
feel sorry for him, and worried also. They seemed more
keen on pinning down who had stolen the objects and
handed them on, then in recovering the treasures. Rudi
strode among the guests, pointing to one thing and another, talking in a low tone or, standing silently as a guest
spoke to him in a learned way about the brushwork, the
pen work, the lines of a sculpture.

Winifred soon became bored, and strolled out. Caroline
was glad to see her go. The atmosphere was strangely
tense in the library, she wanted to concentrate on it, to
puzzle it out. For something curious was definitely going
on.

She had watched art experts work, and she knew they
studied objects for a long time, and even subjected them to
tests. But Wolfgang Gruber could not leave the icon. He
held it in his shaking old hands, muttered to it, turned it
over reverently, returned to gaze at it. But he said nothing
more to Greg or to Caroline about it.

He recognized it, he knew it was authentic, she was
suddenly convinced. Gruber knew that this was the Dorn-

stein Icon, the real icon. But some reason held him silent.
Rudi? Yes, she thought, Rudi had shut him up.

Could it be a plot, a conspiracy? Were they really experts? Yes, she thought they were. The way they spoke of
lines and form, comparing one work against another, the
way they peered and studied and frowned over them, yes,
they were experts. Why, then, this silence? Why did they
not simply say that one object was a Dornstein, another
was not. Or that one was faked, and another real? This
was what Greg wanted sincerely to know. Didn't they realize his earnestness, his intent?

It could only be a plot against him! She became slowly
convinced of that. They could have identified some of the
objects at once. But they did not. They studied, and
frowned, and laid down the drawings, only to return to
them.

Finally Rudi called a halt to the proceedings. "I think it
is about time for lunch. We will leave the objects here, if
you have no objections, Mr. Alpert. All of you may return
here during the next day or two to study further. We wish
to be sure of the identification. You say you do not so far
recognize any of these with certainty as Dornsteins? Well,
I feel sure that some may be. So—we will wait, and
study."

They left it at that. The Bosses drifted away, out to the
gardens, murmuring to each other. The Hintereggers argued briskly with Madame Zollner about a Bellini she had
identified in someone else's collection years ago. It seemed
to have nothing to do with the art which Greg had
brought.

Caroline and Greg went upstairs slowly, staying together
as instinctively as two strange animals in a forest full of
danger. Greg accompanied Caroline to her room. They
stood inside the door, and talked, briefly.

"Something is wrong, Caroline," he said, baldly, a worried frown on his handsome face. He looked his age today.
He was upset, she knew, and worried. "I feel something—
it's in the air—they did know some of the treasures, but
they won't say so. What's wrong?"

"I feel it too, Greg," she told him quietly. "I felt they
did recognize the objects. Especially Herr Gruber. He
knew the Dornstein Icon. He recognized it. He said so.
Then Rudi von Dornstein shut him up. Why? What are
they doing?"

Greg looked down at her face, his mouth twitching, his brown hair mussed, his gray-green eyes rather scared. "You know, Caroline, I hate to say this. But Rudi is unscrupulous. Maybe he's in debt. I know that sounds fantastic. But wealthy people sometimes get in over their heads. Maybe he's tight for money, maybe he just plain doesn't want to pay for the stuff. He would—kill—for those treasures. He is a Dornstein. He feels they are his. And he has the morals of a jungle animal!"

"Oh—no—he would not," she protested faintly.

"I'm afraid he would. Caroline, I wish we could get away, just like that, today. But I can't leave the stuff here. God, and my car is down in that damned village! He has us, all right. Locked up here in the castle with a madman loose. Damn it, they are all mad, living in the past, hating about things that happened more than a quarter of a century ago! Did you hear Madame Zollner going after the Bosses for betraying a friend over thirty years ago in 1942? My god!"

Greg left her to get ready for lunch. Caroline washed her hands, combed her hair, then went down. She sat silently, thinking, thinking painfully.

She did not really believe that Rudi was all that bad. Could she talk to him, discover his intentions? He had seemed honest when he spoke to her. Perhaps she could uncover the mystery. It might be something simple. Perhaps he was merely being over-careful about the identification.

She followed him to his study after lunch. He welcomed her with a smile, set a chair for her. "I won't stay long, I know you are busy," she said timidly.

"You are always welcome, my love," he said, lightly.

She frowned at him, blushing. He only laughed. "I wanted to ask—I just wanted to say. . ." she began to stammer. If only she were not so physically and mentally aware of him! It was difficult to concentrate on what she wanted to say. "Greg is worried that—that the experts are not identifying the objects. Is there no hope? Are they fakes? If so, we are taking up too much time. Greg could be wrong. Even experts can be fooled about art. He sincerely wants to find the right owners."

His eyes had narrowed, he was watching her carefully as she stammered her way through the difficult speech. He came around to her chair, held out his hand to her. Surprised, she put her hand in his, and he drew her up.

"What an earnest, sincere child you are, what an innocent babe, what a little angel," he said, and drew her into his arms. She was so startled, she reacted as she had the first time, she could not struggle.

He pressed his mouth to hers, slowly, gently, then more roughly, as though the touch of her inflamed him. Her hands clung to his arms, trembled at the warmth of his body pressed to hers. Her eyes tight-shut, she received his kisses, and could think no more.

"Little—angel—little warm—angel" he whispered against her cheek, his warm lips roaming from her mouth to her chin to her eyes, to the lobes of her ears. She felt so loved, so adored, she could not move, she could not struggle. This was enchantment, this was desire, this was love, and she could not pull away from it. "Ah—was there—ever—such a pretty—woman—such a lovely—" and he began whispering in German, roughly, words she could barely understand.

Finally, he drew back from her. "Open your eyes, my love," he commanded gently, flicking her cheek with his finger, caressing it with his palm. "Open your eyes. Look at me."

She opened her eyes, dazed, tried to focus on the serious face above hers. He smiled down at her. She could not smile, she was so fascinated, so entranced, so caught up in a daze of warmth and love.

"Tell me the truth," he said, his voice hardening. "I want the truth, Caroline. Are you in on this plot? Do you know which art is real and which is faked? Where did Alpert get the stuff he brought? Tell me the truth!"

She stared up at him, the glow abruptly dying a horrible death. He had romanced her, kissed her, whispered to her—for this. To soften her, to make her say things.

"I don't know," she said, her voice stifled. "I don't know anything except that Greg Alpert is the kindest man I have ever known and you the most cruel! He has been good to me and you would deceive . . ." She wrenched herself away from him.

He could have held her, but he did not. He let her go, watching her steadily, a curious light in his eyes. "You will tell me the truth, Caroline, my dear," he said. "You will tell me just what his game is."

"Game! His game is art! He loves art!" she cried. "And he is generous! He wants to give back the stolen art and you—you can't understand anyone like that! In your world, everyone grabs and steals for himself! It is man against man! You can't comprehend someone who is generous and giving! Who loves art more than money! You don't understand a man like that!"

"No, I can't understand a man like that," he said. She stared at him, at the cynical curve of the mouth that had so recently touched hers with such tenderness.

Fake tenderness. He had done this to make her talk! What she was supposed to say, she did not know. But she understood him now. He was so sure of his own charm, that he thought he could use it as the Nazis used their instruments of torture—to wring out true and false confessions.

She turned and ran from the room, running blindly up the stairs to her bedroom. He ran after her, then stopped at the foot of the stairway. She paused at the top, glared down at him, until tears blurred her eyes. Then she ran on to her room.

She thought he had said her name sharply. She did not turn back. She slammed the door and locked it, and leaned against it.

Flight. That was all she could think of. Flight. She must leave, if she had to walk to Vienna.

She went over to her large traveling handbag, the one Denise had given her because it would "hold everything." She gathered her few pieces of jewelry, crammed them and a few other items—a change of stockings, money, passport—inside.

She worked in a frenzy. She knew she had to get away, from Rudi, from his ruthlessness, his charm, his coldness, his hate, his passions that she did not understand. She had to run away from herself, she thought, from her weakness over Rudi.

She packed her small cosmetic case, which she could carry easily, with a dress, then put on her sweater and light white coat. Now, she was ready.

She peered out the windows, but she could see little. It was a dull afternoon, cloudy, a little cooler than yesterday. She knew the guests would be wandering about on their own. Countess von Dornstein often spent part of the afternoon consulting with her household. Rudi often rode out.

She went quietly to the hallway, opened the door, listened. No sound. She made for the backstairs, crept down them. She was in the back hall across from the kitchen. All was quiet.

She ought to tell Greg, but what could she say to him?

She was swept with the overwhelming desire to get away from everyone. She just wanted to be alone, to think, to recover.

She ran out the back door, through the kitchen gardens, around the castle, creeping through the tall grasses, out past the horse stables and currying yards, down the long hills beyond.

She walked and walked. She had not realized it was so far. The village could not even be seen from the hills where she was. She thought she was on the right road. She did not attempt to follow the road, as it wound and twisted back on itself. She ran down slopes, steeply graded, down the slick grass, sliding, stumbling, falling down again and again, but going on, persisting, running away from something she did not understand.

Behind her, she suddenly heard the sounds of a horse's hoofs and a voice calling, "Caroline! Caroline!" She turned, saw Rudi riding on the huge black stallion, and was pierced by terror.

She ran blindly, dropping the case, running, running. She stumbled and fell on the slope, sliding to the bottom. The horse came up to her, she gazed up frightened into Rudi's frowning face. He slid from the horse, bent over her.

"No!" she cried out sharply as he tried to pick her up. "No! Let me go! I must go!"

"Caroline, you are insane! What are you doing?" He picked her up, shook her like a child, brushed her off with hard hands. "Where did you think you were going?"

"Home" she said, and began to weep against his green leather coat. "I want to go home!"

She was crying now, helplessly, worn out and scared to death. He picked her up, carried her over to a car. He spoke sharply to the man driving, who jumped out, and held the door for Rudi. Rudi tucked Caroline into the front seat, got in beside her. He flung further orders at the man in German.

"You silly girl," he said to Caroline. "This is your home now. You belong to me, don't you know that?"

She did not even attempt to understand him. She rubbed her hands over her face, not caring that her hands were covered with dirt and grass. "Let me go," she said wearily, huskily, her throat paining her more than ever. "Let me go, I must go—back to Vienna—back home."

He paid no attention to her words. His jaw was hard-set, his eyebrows scowling. He looked so cold that she shrank back in the seat, her hands pressed together. She had lost her case, her pocketbook. She was covered with dirt, and she felt utterly foolish and miserable.

Rudi drove up to the side of the castle, not the front. He helped her out, took her by a side door. She thought he was ashamed of her and did not want the guests to see her. But he took her up a stairway that was new to her, to a wing she did not know. He opened a door, took her inside. She glanced around, beginning to wake from a daze.

"This is not—my room—my room," she stammered.

"This is your new room," he said curtly, frowning. "I will send for Trudi. Wash and change. Sleep if you like. You will remain here for a time, until you are sensible."

"Where am I?" she whispered, staring up at him, truly frightened now. "I want to see Greg."

"You are in my wing of the castle. I will take care of you. No, you cannot see Greg. I will return later, and we will talk."

And he went out abruptly, slamming the door. She heard distinctly the turning of the key as he locked the door after him. Now she was really a prisoner.

Chapter 8

Caroline sat and waited, for what, she did not know. When the door was unlocked, she looked up fearfully. But it was only Trudi, dear familiar Trudi, in her black dress and her neat white apron. She came in, rustled over to Caroline, bent over her compassionately.

Another maid followed her, carrying some of Caroline's clothes. A man brought in her suitcases, including her handbag and cosmetic case.

Trudi gently made Caroline undress, made her wash in the new bathroom, put on her nightgown and robe. Caroline submitted, in a daze. She was very weary, shaking from her terror and her flight. She felt physically exhausted, mentally unable to cope.

Trudi turned back the bedcovers, and indicated that Caroline was to sleep. She brought a glass. Caroline thought it was water, and she was thirsty. She began to drink, then paused. It had an odd taste.

"What is—" she began. The woman gently forced the glass back to her lips.

"Drink, little one. Drink." Caroline drank it, and her brain began to go round and round. She felt dizzy, and frightened all over again. Something had been in that drink.

She tried to protest feebly. "What was in—that drink—Trudi—what—"

"Sleep, little one." The big rough hand caressed her forehead, forced her gently back against the pillows. The door opened, Rudi came in, as though he had a right to do so. Caroline blinked at him, her vision seemed to be blurring in a frightening way.

"Rudi," she said. "The drink—drink."

"Did she drink it all?" he asked Trudi, crisply, his gaze looking down impersonally at Caroline in the huge bed.

"Yes, sir, all of it," said Trudi.

"Good." He sat down at the side of the bed. Caroline knew she should protest, but her tongue seemed to have thickened, her throat still pained her. She could not speak, only stare at him in numb terror.

His hand stroked back her hair, he said to her quietly, "You will sleep now, Caroline. You will sleep and rest. When you waken, you will do as I wish. You will do as I command you. Do you hear me? Just nod your head if you hear me."

Slowly she nodded her head, moving it on the pillows. "Good. You will listen to me, and you will go to sleep as I am talking. When you waken, you will do as I wish. You will do everything that I wish."

His voice was quiet, slow, deliberate, hypnotic. Caroline realized it, but could do nothing about it. Her limbs seemed paralyzed, she could not move. The drug, she thought. She had been drugged. Her brain was blurring even more, the terror remained, but not the will to fight against him. In the back of her mind she knew a dull terror. She wanted to fight against him, to scream, but she could not even whisper.

His hand stroked her head lightly, rhythmically. "You will sleep, now, Caroline. You will sleep. You will close your eyes and sleep. Close your eyes and sleep."

She wanted to keep her eyes wide open, but she could not. Her eyes closed, slowly, flickered, then closed, as though pasted shut. She heard his voice, fading away.

"When you—waken—you will—do—just as I say—you will do what I tell you. Caroline, you are under my will now. You will do as I say. Nod your head if you understand me."

She was almost beyond moving. But she knew she must

nod her head. Her head moved—slowly, a fraction of an inch.

"Good," he murmured. "Good. You will sleep—now—sleep—"

And she slept with the murmur of his deep voice in her ear, the touch of his hand gently smoothing her forehead.

When she slowly wakened, she did not remember where she was. It was dusk, and she could not see the room clearly. It was a huge room, in green and gold, not like her other room. Where was she? Dornstein, she vaguely remembered. Dornstein. Where in Dornstein?

Prisoner. She remembered that word, groping in the mists that seemed to hide her thoughts.

Prisoner. Art. Greg. Greg?

"She is awake," someone whispered.

"Ah, yes." It was Rudi's voice. He came closer to the bed, leaned over her. "Caroline, you are awake, and now you will do as I wish. Nod your head if you understand."

She wanted to fight him. She frowned, struggled against the numbing effect of the drug. He was holding a glass to her lips. She tried to turn her head away.

"Drink this. You will feel better," he said, and held her head while she drank, unwillingly. The blur began to cover her mind again. He had drugged her once more. Oh, God, she thought, in dull terror. What would happen to her?

The voices murmured on. A lamp was lighted, and she saw a white dress lying across a chair. A white brocade dress covered with precious lace. It looked beautiful, like a wedding dress, she thought, dimly. Why a wedding dress?

Rudi bent over her again, and said, "Trudi will dress you. Then I will come for you. You will do and say as I direct you. Do you understand me? You will obey me? You will say yes to whatever I ask? Nod your head."

She struggled, but could not defy him. Her head nodded, her wide violet eyes gazed up at him, seeing him only dimly, the sharp black eyes, the lean tanned face, the hard mouth.

"Good. Trudi—" And he went away, after saying some things in German to the two women. Trudi and another maid came over to her, helped her rise from the bed. She felt weak and helpless, they had to hold her up at first.

She was washed, then dressed in fragile lace underclothing. Then the white antique lace dress was held for her to slip her arms into, and then it was pulled over her head, drawn down, so she was a prisoner inside it, in the white brocade and lace—a prisoner—that rang a bell in her mind, and she wanted to struggle. But she could not.

The dress was pulled down. She stared at herself in the full-length mirror, the tall, slim, blonde-haired young woman with wide violet eyes, being dressed in a long antique wedding dress. Trudi murmured her satisfaction, patting the dress into place, fastening the many buttons with care.

Then another maid brought the wedding veil, a long white cloud, and they laid it on her hair, and down over her shoulders, arranging the folds with care. Trudi fastened her pearl necklace her parents had given her, and set the earrings in her ears. Now she brought a bracelet of gold and pearls and jade which Caroline had never seen before.

She stared at it, frowning in puzzlement.

Trudi said gently, "This is from the Dornstein jewels. For you, for the wedding day." And she set on her right hand a large emerald ring, set in gold. Green and gold, green and gold, thought Caroline. The Dornstein colors. Rudi often wore forest green and gold, they were his colors.

Then Rudi came in, and stared at her. He did not speak for a long moment. She could not speak either, she was so drugged.

"Caroline," he murmured, and took her cold hand in his. He chafed it gently between his two hands. "Listen to me, darling. We are going to be married. I will take care of you always. Take care of you, do you understand?"

She nodded her head, though she did not understand. She stared at him wonderingly through the cobweb of lace covering her face. If only she could think clearly, if only she could speak.

"Say, yes, Caroline," he was urging her.

She cleared her throat huskily. "Yes," she managed.

"I have explained to the priest that you have hurt your throat. He will not expect you to say anything but yes. You answer when I tell you. Come now." And he took her arm, then held her by the waist as she could not seem to move.

With Trudi on one side helping her, and Rudi holding her on the other, Caroline was led out into the hallway, down a long narrow stairway, down and down and down.

Chill struck her, as they reached the lowest level. They were not in the main part of the castle, she finally realized. She felt terror strike her again.

All about her were tombs. She saw inscriptions, now faded and dimmed by age. The Dornstein family tombs. She was in the tombs. Another chill struck through her, and she shuddered convulsively. Rudi's arm tightened.

"Only a little time, darling," he whispered in her ear.

"Rudi, help me," she managed to plead. He frowned.

Near despair, even in her drugged state, she let them lead her where they would. And they came to a dimly lighted chapel with more tombs lining the walls. There was a white cloth on the altar, the Dornstein icon was set near the cross. A smiling priest stood waiting in white robes. The countess, in a beautiful gown of blue silk, was also there.

The countess smiled. Caroline stared at her. How could she pretend to be so friendly and kind, when her own son was carrying out this grim farce? For she believed now it was a farce, for what reason she did not know.

He was pretending to marry her, here in this cold stone crypt. Why was Rudi pretending to marry her? For what purpose? Why did he pretend to be so gentle with her, when he could crush her with his lean strong fingers?

He held her with his arm about her waist as they faced the priest. Only the countess was there, and a few servants. She heard a murmur at the back of the small room, but Rudi held her so she could not turn around.

Where was Greg? Had they killed him? Where were the other guests? Were they ignorant of this, or did they let von Dornstein do as he pleased? Why would he marry her, even in pretense, when he wanted Winifred, the long leggy blonde with the cold green eyes?

The priest was speaking. Rudi pressed her waist gently, and directed her attention to what the man was saying. But it was in Latin and German, and she could not make her drugged brain comprehend. It sounded like a religious ceremony, she thought it might even be a wedding ceremony. But how could it be?

Rudi was saying something, repeating some words. Then he whispered to her, "Say yes, Caroline."

"Yes," she muttered.

There was a little pause. He told her another time to say the word yes, and she did. A ring was put on her left hand, a gold band that felt heavy to her. Then Rudi put another ring beside it, a single blazing diamond set with two emeralds. He led her hand to put a single gold band on his hand, only it was on his right hand. Dimly she remembered that German people wore the wedding band on their right hands. Then why were hers on the left? She gazed at her hands, in puzzled wonder.

Rudi whispered, "I told the priest it was the American custom to wear them on the left."

She nodded, stupidly. It was probably part of the act he was putting on. But why such lengths? And for what witnesses? She saw only the countess and a few servants. Then it seemed to be over. Rudi gently put back the wedding veil, took her in his arms, and pressed his warm lips to her chilled ones. She could not respond. He gazed down anxiously at her face, then kissed her again, lightly, and let her go.

The countess rustled up to her. ""My dearest Caroline," she said, and there were tears in the bright black eyes. She leaned forward, cupped Caroline's face tenderly between her hands, and kissed her on each cheek, then on the lips. "My dearest daughter. How I will love you! You are perfect for my Rudi."

Caroline looked at her in bewilderment. Was this part of the plot, or was the countess deceived? She moved her lips, tried to speak. Rudi turned her gently away from his mother, to indicate the servants.

Each one came up, knelt to her, kissed her left hand, and her right. They muttered words in German, Trudi had tears in her eyes. Then as she turned once more, she saw the madman. He and his guard, Kurt of the scarred face, were standing at the back of the chapel.

The thin, white-haired man was holding on to Kurt's arm. As Rudi and Caroline walked slowly to the back of the chapel, he leaned forward, his brillant black eyes shining. He was like a child, a small intent child, and Caroline managed to smile at him gently, pitying, remembering his terrible past, the torments he had known. He gazed at her, then smiled back sweetly. Then they were past him, and out into the other part of the cellars.

The countess followed them out, her full blue gown sweeping majestically on the cellar floor. She said something sharply to Rudi in German.

He said no to her, and shook his head abruptly. He

turned Caroline toward the stairs. The countess spoke
again, pleadingly. Rudi shook his head, spoke more gently
in German. Caroline could not follow the conversation at
all.

Then Rudi said to her, "We will dine in my suite, Caroline. I want to be alone with my bride."

She was confused. Was he going to carry out this non-
sense even further? What did he hope to gain? She wanted
again to protest, or to scream. But her throat would not
work, her brain could not communicate any definite orders
to her vocal cords.

So he led her up the stairs again, up and up. She was
dizzy from the many turnings and twistings, but it did
seem they were going to some other room. He led her
along corridors, long and lined with ancestral portraits and
scenes of the hills around Dornstein.

Then he opened a door, and led her inside. She could
not go further than a few steps. She had to stop and stare,
even though her vision was blurred with the drug.

The room was huge and glorious with color. An enormous crystal chandelier hung from the high ceiling, and
blazed with light. The room was in green and gold, the sofas were upholstered in green velvet. The chairs covered in
a matching green and gold brocade. Little gilt tables were
scattered about and carelessly strewn with boxes and statuettes and precious objects.

And beyond was an opened door. Through it she could
see an equally huge bedroom, also in green and gold. A
huge canopied bed, with green canopy, green velvet bed-
spread. A servant was wheeling into the sitting room an
enormous table covered with a white cloth, silver serving
dishes and exquisite china plates.

Behind her, Rudi was removing the white veil from her
head. "Welcome my bride," he said softly, and she felt his
hands fall possessively on her shoulders.

Chapter 9

Several servants served the elaborate dinner. Partly from the strain, partly from the drugs, Caroline was not hungry. Rudi made little pretense of eating either, merely tasting one dish or another, urging her to try something.

But there was a tension between them which was not dispelled even by the excellent champagne. Rudi sat beside her on a green velvet sofa, and every time he moved he seemed to touch her, on her arm, her hand, her knee, her thigh. She was burningly conscious of him, of his look, his touch, of the strange situation he had created.

She kept fighting to clear her mind, to puzzle things out. A gray mist seemed to cloud her brain, she could not manage to clarify anything. She had a feeling she wanted to relax and let Rudi take charge, but she kept striving against it. He was an enemy, a prison guard, she kept reminding herself.

It was difficult to remember when Rudi's voice lowered to a husky murmur, when his eyes sought hers in tender query, when his fingers touched hers in handing her a glass. It was impossible to remain on guard against him. She remembered that she had begun to love him, before this had happened. Was she afraid of him? Or in love with him?

Rudi finally sent away the remains of the dinner and dismissed the servants. Trudi was in the bedroom laying out a white nightgown of silk and lace, a matching negligee, white slippers. Where had they come from, she wondered.

Rudi leaned back against the cushions. He was watching her. She sat silently, her hands nervously clasping each other. Her white brocade and lace gown, where had it come from? It smelled slightly musty, as though it had been laid away for a long time.

"This gown," she began, touching it. "Where did it come from? The fit . . ."

"It was my mother's and her mother's before her," he said. "You are just her size, when she was married."

She frowned directly at him. "I cannot understand . . ."

He interrupted. "Do not try to understand now, Caroline. I will explain everything to you eventually." He was so autocratic that she frowned more heavily. Her indignation made the effect of the drug lift for a moment.

"You are being very high-handed! I never agreed to marry you! And where is Greg? Why wasn't he at the wedding, if it was a wedding!"

He put his hand gently, lightly, on her knee. The touch seemed to burn through her gown.

"It was a wedding, our wedding, in the family chapel. You are wearing the family wedding gown. And as for agreeing, you did agree. You said yes at all the proper times! I have witnesses!"

She thought he was laughing at her. She turned, glared at him, to meet the burning expression in his eyes, the intimate look that made her flush and look away hastily. She finally moved away from him and stood up. He stood with her, courteously.

"Here is Trudi, ready to serve you. Go with her, Caroline," he said gently.

She had intended to berate him, to demand answers, once away from the closeness of the sofa. But he took her gently by the shoulders and pushed her toward the bedroom door. Trudi was indeed waiting there, smiling.

Caroline went into the bedroom with her, and Trudi closed the door. The maid did not speak, for which Caroline was thankful. She was more dizzy than ever, from the drugs and champagne and little food. She kept pressing her hand to her forehead. Was she in a dream or a nightmare? Was she sane or insane? What was happening to her? Nothing seemed real, nothing was clear. The world was an ureal blur, only Rudi, and his presence beyond that door, was frighteningly real.

Trudi unfastened the beautiful white wedding gown, laid it on a chair. She undressed Caroline, because she felt quite incapable of moving. She swayed on her feet, Trudi caught her and murmured something comforting in German.

The maid put on her the white lace nightgown, the matching negligee, the little white mules. Caroline wondered again where they had come from. They looked new and fresh. But she had not brought them with her from Vienna. Had Rudi sent for them? When? Had he been so sure of her? Oh, no, he had not planned this in advance. It had been an impulse—even if it was all part of a game, a play, some trick he was playing on her.

She wondered again, wearily, her hand on her forehead, what he meant to gain with this elaborate show. Why his mother at a mock wedding? Why use the family wedding gown? Why did he insist they were really married? The priest had seemed real, but men could play dress-up if they wished.

She sighed deeply. Trudi tucked her into bed, brushed back her loose hair, murmured over her, and left her. Caroline closed her eyes, the drugs taking a firm hold of her now that she was lying down. It would be so easy—to fall asleep—to drift off into the haze—

Someone was moving in the bedroom. She forced her heavy eyelids to open, saw Rudi tall and strange in a dark green robe walking across to a lamp. He leaned forward to turn it off, and she saw his dark face a moment, saturnine and hard, in the brief light before it was switched off. She caught her breath in alarm.

The room was dim now, there was only one small light near the door left burning. Rudi came to the bed, and removed his robe. He tossed it on a nearby gold chair, and stood in his pajamas. He stood there thoughtfully for a long moment, looking down at her speculatively.

She stared up at him.

He finally slid into bed beside her. "Your eyes are so large and so violet-blue, my sweet," he whispered, and bent over her. Slowly he pressed his lips first to one eyelid, then to the other. He closed her eyes for her, and she could not seem to open them again.

She felt his arms moving about her, to lift her, and draw her close to him, under him. He lifted one of her arms around his neck. It lay there passively, where he had moved it. He bent his head, and she felt his lips on her cheek, her mouth, her chin, below to her neck where the lace gown fell away. He kissed her throat, and his lips began to grow hotter and more demanding.

One overwhelming question loomed in her blurred mind.

"Rudi—why, why?" she finally whispered, as his hand began to roam over her body, moving from her arm to her shoulder, down to her breasts. "Why?"

"I love you," he whispered, and his lips pressed to the soft hollow of her throat.

She sighed. It was like a game, she thought. She saw and heard all the moves and the clues—but she could not put them together to make any sense.

What was the use of fighting? He was stronger—and she was drugged. She could not fight him. Her arm curled closer about his head, began to move of its own volition. When he kissed her lips again, she responded shyly, her lips moving slightly under his, questioningly, wonderingly.

"Darling—Caroline—my love . . ." He kissed her harder, his lips open against hers. His hand cupped her bare breast inside the lace, and she caught her breath at the touch.

She had never known a man, she had shied off from their caresses, and so everything he did was new to her. The soft pressure of his hand on her breast, the way his lips moved on her throat and shoulder, the way his leg moved to lie on hers, his overpowering approach to her.

She knew what would happen, but it had been so clinically described in her college texts that she was quite unprepared for the rapture and strangeness, the pain and ecstasy mingled, of his contact with her. When he took her, she cried out, clutched at him and tried to push him away, until he calmed her again.

Then he took her again, more slowly and gently, and went on to the finish. And this time his caresses and the way he moved with her were so overwhelming, that she could not keep from responding. Her hands closed behind his head, holding him to her breast, and her body moved under his, striving with his. She was half-crying, now, but with pleasure.

At the height, he whispered, demandingly, "Tell me you love me. Caroline, tell me—"

She moved her head on the pillow, dreamily.

"Tell me! Caroline, say I love you!"

"I—love . . ." She hesitated, reluctance and shyness mingling.

"Say it!"

"I—love—you—I—love—you—ooohhhh!" She ended in a surprised whisper as he rewarded her with a movement that sent ecstasy racing through her. She fell back against the pillow. Her fists clenched, relaxed, clenched, relaxed, and she sighed deeply as the strange sensations rippled through her.

He drew her gently back into his arms when it was over.

"Sleep now, darling. Sleep," he whispered, and stroked her blonde hair back over his shoulder as she lay with her face buried in his chest. She was trembling, and she felt he was shaking also.

She wakened twice in the night, but only briefly. She felt him move as she stirred, and he drew her closer to him. She muttered something, went back to sleep, feeling oddly safe and secure in his arms.

When she wakened in the morning, it was because he was distributing little nibbling, teasing kisses across her face and throat. She opened her eyes, stared blankly at him, unable to remember where she was. When she remembered, she began to blush furiously, because she was completely naked in his bed, and he was smiling knowingly down at her, and his hand was on her.

The sunshine was streaming across the blanket from the tall casement windows. It was reflected from the gold tables and chairs, the shining mirrors on the walls, the crystal chandelier. She looked at his hand as it caressed her, the sunshine touching the dark hairs, turning their tips to gold. His black curly head was bent to her body, and she felt his lips moving over her.

"It was a dream," she thought. "I am awake, but I am still dreaming. I dreamed that he loved me that last night we were married—and he slept with me."

But it was not a dream. She was here with him, and he was kissing her with lazy absorption. The haze seemed to have lifted from her mind.

"Rudi, I want you to tell me," she began with some determination. "Tell me what happened, why you went through that ceremony of marriage with me. Why? Why?"

He lifted his head. The dreaminess left his face, it seemed to harden and his eyes narrowed, as though to shut his thoughts from her. "We did get married, Caroline," he said definitely. "It was a real marriage. Why comes later. When you are ready to hear." He moved, left the bed, reached for his robe, and belted it about himself. He lifted the sheets and placed them securely about her, drew up the blanket.

"I want to hear now, Rudi. I want to know . . ." she was beginning. He seemed to pay no attention to her.

"Rest, sleep. I'll send Trudi to you later. Order what you want for breakfast. I'll return later, I have some work I must do this morning—yes, even on our wedding morning, when I would prefer to remain with you." Smiling, deliberately, he bent and kissed her mouth. Her lips did not move. She watched him steadily as he rose again.

Yes, it was an act. He was pretending everything was normal and usual—when it was not at all.

He went to a smaller room on the other side of the living room. She heard his voice, and the softer deferential voice of his valet Lothar. They talked, then both were silent, and she heard doors closing.

She was restless, she wanted to try to find Greg and talk to him. Surely he could help her figure it out, help her get away. She got up cautiously, found only the white gown and negligee to wear. Everything, including the white wedding dress, had been taken away. There were no clothes in the closets. She grimaced. A silken prison. They did not mean to let her escape.

She put on the gown and negligee, and went to the living room. As soon as she opened the door, Trudi jumped up from where she waited, and beamed at her. She came toward her. Caroline hesitated. She did not want to attack Trudi, kind middle-aged Trudi who had been good to her.

"My clothes, Trudi, where are they?" she asked quietly.

"Yes, yes, presently. You are hungry, no? You ate so

little last night, the excitement. Let me bring you egg, bacon, biscuits, some jam? Some coffee, yes?"

Caroline sighed. It was like fighting a featherdown puff. And she was hungry. "All right, Trudi."

The maid flew away—and locked the door after her. Caroline set her mouth, but she was scared inside. She went to the huge bathroom, and washed, finding her own toothbrush and toothpaste residing in a mirrored cupboard beside some obviously belonging to Rudi. She touched his shaving utensils curiously, gravely. She had never lived intimately with a man before. Even at home, she had had her own little bathroom and bedroom, in a different wing from that of her parents. What would marriage be like?

Or would she even have the chance to find out? Was it really all a farce?

What was Rudi's purpose? What did he hope to gain from all this? He had understood her questions, he had said he would tell her why when she was ready to hear. But he was ready now—and he would not tell her.

Trudi brought her breakfast, then mysteriously produced Caroline's suitcases, and proceeded to unpack them. Caroline was relieved, but also very puzzled to see her own dresses and possessions appearing in Trudi's hands. Was she wrong again, to think they would keep her prisoner without any clothes in which to escape? Evidently so.

She did notice that the doors were carefully locked and unlocked each time Trudi or one of the maids and servants came and went. The keys resided in one of Trudi's capacious pockets.

Caroline ate hungrily, and felt much better. Her body ached somewhat, but she decided philosophically that it would have done so even if she had had a conventional marriage. That was what happened on a wedding night. And Rudi had not really hurt her, he had been very tender and gentle. She sipped her coffee, thick with whipped cream the way she had learned to enjoy it, and thought seriously about Rudi.

Her brain was much clearer today. She began puzzling out what might have happened. It was definitely related to Greg, and to the art treasures. And probably to her attempt to run away.

Was that what had set things off? Her running away? Had Rudi decided that the only way to keep her at the castle was to marry her? Her eyebrows drew together, she paused in her drinking to ponder.

"Water, Miss Caroline," said Trudi, but Caroline shook her head. The water was slightly clouded, and she remembered the way she had been drugged the day before.

Trudi set down the glass on her tray, and offered her more coffee. Caroline accepted it, added the thick cream, and sat to drink a while.

"What would you like to wear, Miss Caroline?" asked Trudi. "This lilac outfit?" She said the words just the way Caroline had taught her.

"Yes, I believe so . . ." Caroline hesitated, rubbed her forehead. Was it her imagination, or was she feeling rather drowsy again?

The door opened with a click of the lock, and Rudi walked in. He was frowning. His expression relaxed when he saw Caroline sitting there in her white negligee.

He came over at once, bent and kissed her cheek, then her lips, and smiled down at her. "Beautiful. How are you, my love?"

"I'm fine," she said, though she was beginning to feel dizzy again. Trudi discreetly left the room, and began moving about the bedroom, airing the bed, opening the windows.

He sat down beside her, took one hand in his palm, turned it to look at it and the ring on it thoughtfully.

"I want to talk to you, Rudi," she said, quietly, when he was silent. "I want to see Greg. I want an explanation of why you have treated me as you have!" In spite of her resolution, her voice rose.

He glanced at the tray, noticed the full glass of water. "Not now, Caroline. Not today. I want you to remain in these rooms, quietly, and trust me."

"Trust you! Trust you—after the way you made me marry you! Yes, I know I said yes, but I was drugged! What possible explanation . . ."

He lifted the glass and offered it to her. "I want you to drink this." He put it to her lips. She pushed it away, turned her head.

"No. I want to talk to you. I won't be drugged again! Where is Greg? Is he dead? Why do you want to take the art from him without paying for it? You have the money, it isn't as though he were asking an extravagant amount.

You should be glad to get the icon back—it is the true Dornstein Icon, I know that from the way your mother reacted, and Mr. Gruber. They knew it—they knew the icon at once."

Her voice was shrill and excited. She felt nervous and distraught as the drugs began to take hold and she could feel her mind blurring. Trudi had drugged her, she knew it. She resisted fiercely as Rudi held the glass to her lips.

"No—no—no—I won't—"

"Yes, you must, Caroline. You are too excited. I want you to be calm and quiet, and to talk to me later. We shall talk, I promise you, for you have much to tell me about Mr. Alpert and his operations . . ."

He held her head, suddenly, roughly, and forced the glass to her lips. He held her in such a way, that she had to drink from it, draining it at his insistence. She felt sanity slipping from her, he was so rough and bullying, when before he had been so gentle. She wanted to cry. He didn't love her, he didn't really love her, he could not, if he made her drink this drug, if he did this.

She did not understand—Mr. Alpert and his operations—

"No—I do not know," she said faintly, and fell back against the cushions with a heavy sigh of regret. The blackness was closing in on her, more intensely than before, much more intensely. She was afraid—with a dull terror.

She heard the rustle of a heavy dress, Trudi's dress, her voice exclaiming in German, raised in alarm.

Rudi answered curtly. "No, no," said Trudi, "I put it in the coffee."

"My God!" Rudi said. "The coffee—but I made her drink the water . . ."

They argued in German, she could not get the words. The blackness had taken over. She could not move. Rudi's arm went around her, he raised her up, but she fell back as soon as he released her.

"Darling, Caroline—oh, God, we both gave you—oh, God, darling, don't go to sleep—stay awake, where is the antidote—oh, God, we gave you too much! My darling—oh, God—God!"

The anguish in his voice surprised her vaguely, but she was too far gone to heed it. She sighed, faintly, and fell over, blacking out completely.

Just before she lost consciousness, she knew the worst terror of her life. The man she had married, the man she loved, had drugged her forcefully—to this. To death? Was this death?

Chapter 10

Caroline seemed to be returning from a long journey. She had walked and walked for so many miles that her body ached, her legs ached, her head ached. She sighed, moved, turned her head on—what? A soft pillow, a soft bed. But her arms could scarcely move, they felt heavy and useless.

"She moves," said a voice in German, Trudi's voice. Someone came over to the bed, and she caught the scent of the shaving lotion Rudi used.

"Darling, Caroline," he said quietly. His lips brushed her aching forehead. "Can you open your eyes, love? Open your eyes. Open them."

She must open her eyes—she could not. The lashes fluttered, could not open.

"Try again, love, open you eyes. Open them, love." His voice was tender. His hand slowly stroked her aching shoulders. His touch—when he made love—it had been so very sweet—she wanted to come back—to him—wanted to come back—from the long dark journey.

She forced her eyes to open, but could not focus them at first. She finally frowned, blinked, managed to see his face swim in and out of focus, back in again. The hard dark face, concerned now, the black eyes worried.

"That's it, darling. You can see me, can't you?"

She finally nodded, lifted one hand feebly. "I—ache," she managed to whisper.

"We'll let you rest and sleep now. It's all right, love. You can sleep now. You won't slip away from me." His voice roughened and deepened.

She sighed, and closed her eyes again. She slept, feeling his hand stroking hers gently, hearing his voice rumbling softly in her ears.

When she wakened, it was dark. Through the opened door, she could see lights in the living room, and hear someone there. She managed to call, "Trudi?"

The maid came in at once, turned on one of the lights, and beamed down at her. "You are awake, at last, ah, good, good."

Caroline moved cautiously. The ache was still there, but not so bad now. Her mind was still blurry, she did not want to think.

Trudi brought her some tea and crackers, which was all Caroline wanted. She ate, slept again, a long deep sleep. She was vaguely aware once in the night that Rudi was there in bed with her, near her, but not touching.

When she wakened, late in the morning, he was not there, but the imprint of his head was on the pillow next to hers. She stretched, yawned, glad that the blurriness was almost gone. But worries began to close in on her as she was able to think again. What were they doing to her? And why, why, why?

She kept coming back to the art. She lay very quietly, as sunlight streamed across the bed, and tried to think of any and every detail that might help her solve the puzzle.

Presently Trudi came in, helped her get up and bathe. She was dressed in a blue linen dress with matching blue sweater.

She ate breakfast, drank her coffee, wondered if it was drugged. She could not fight them, she thought. If they chose to drug her, they would. She waited to see if her brain would blur, but to her intense relief it did not.

The door was locked after the servant had removed the breakfast table. Trudi was humming as she moved about in the bedroom. Caroline discovered a wide window seat with a soft covering of green velvet, half-hidden behind the drawn curtains, and she curled up there to gaze out at the scene below.

This was a different section of the huge castle from where her other room had been. As she peered out the long casement windows, she could see a rolling valley and hills beyond. She wondered if that might be Hungary beyond, and thought it was in that direction. She gazed, dreamily, thinking of the Tartars, the Turks, all the invaders who had sought to crush Dornstein, and been thrown back by the ancestors of the man who had married her— who had pretended to marry her—or really married her . . .

Her mind turned impatiently from that puzzle.

She peered down directly below her. They seemed to be on the second floor. Below was a large garden she had not seen before. It was surrounded on two sides by high walls, on the third side by the castle itself, and on the fourth side, a sheer cliff dropped to the valley floor. This must be the side of the volcano that Greg had mentioned in Vienna, when he had told her the castle was perched on cliffs that could not be scaled.

"Only an eagle could get up. They used to hurl their enemies down those cliffs to death on the rocks below," he had told her dramatically, and she had shuddered.

There was no escape. She became more depressed as she sat there. She did not know why she was a prisoner, what was wanted from her.

"Caroline?" Caroline started at the deep voice, and crouched instinctively in the window seat.

It was Rudi. He said her name again. She bit her lips. It was foolish to hide. She pushed back the heavy velvet curtain and said, "Yes, I am here."

He turned, he had been walking about the room, and there was surprise on his face as he saw her sitting there in the window. The sunshine was warming her, and he was looking at the brightness of her hair against the casement windows.

"Oh, you look . . ." he hesitated, then ended with a little laugh. "You will be tired of hearing this, Caroline. You look like an angel—only today you are an angel in a stained glass window." He went over to her as she sat there, looking up at him, her long legs curled under her blue skirt. He bent over her, cupped her chin in one hand, then slowly bent and kissed her lips. It was a curiously gentle kiss, yet she sensed passion held in hard check.

He straightened up, and looked down at her, but she kept her eyes stubbornly lowered. She did not want to look at him, to be confused by him. And she knew she was flushed and disturbed by that kiss. He seemed so—possessive—she thought. And she believed the marriage was a fake, no matter what he said.

"Come over here," he said, clasping her hand and pulling her up. She went with him. He drew her over to the couch, sat down beside her "I want to talk to you. You said you began working for Mr. Alpert about three months ago." And he began quizzing her all over again about the way Greg Alpert worked, who his associates were, how long she had known him.

She replied patiently, but cautiously. Rudi was trying to find out something, perhaps to trick Greg into giving him the icon and the rest of the art. She felt indignant again at the shabby treatment Greg was getting. He had worked so hard to put the collection together, he had put his own money into it, had paid for the icon and asked no questions. He had wanted only to restore it to its rightful owner, and how ungrateful and dreadful Rudi was acting about it!

"Does Greg Alpert work alone?" Rudi returned to that subject again and again. "Does he have an associate?"

"Well, freelance artists bring their work for him to sell. That's the way the business works. I don't know why you keep asking! I have told you . . ."

He held her hand, to calm her, she thought with some anger. She tried to pull it away, but he held her hand easily in his big one. "I want to know if he has any friends close to him in the business."

"No," she said shortly, trying again to pull her hand away. He held it, though it became painful to her. She bit her lips. He didn't really care if he hurt her or not.

"No relatives?"

She hesitated, about to say no. "Well, I don't . . ."

"Who?" he asked sharply, looking down into her face.

"Well, I think he has a brother. I mean—the man is—well—I don't know."

"Tell me about the brother," said Rudi quietly, urgently. His hand was cruelly tight.

"You are hurting my hand," she said finally.

He stared down at their joined hands, blinked, as though he had not realized what he was doing. He loosened his grip. "I'm sorry, Caroline. But tell me about the brother."

"I don't really know much. But a man came to the gallery twice, and he said—well, he might have been joking. You know how people say they are soul brothers, all that. He might have meant . . ."

"Tell me about the man."

She frowned, trying to remember. "He did look something like Greg, but he was much older. And Greg did say his brother was seriously wounded in Germany in World War II. Greg was bitter about it. He said his brother was treated badly. Maybe as a prisoner of war, I don't know. He was very upset one day, and had been drinking. Oh, he doesn't often drink, believe me! He is the nicest guy."

"The brother. He looked like Alpert? Was his name Alpert?"

"Well, no. I mean, Greg said something about one of them changing his name, being adopted—was that it?"

"What was his name?"

"I don't know. I didn't hear it clearly. I wasn't really introduced. I was just coming back from lunch and the man was leaving, and he smiled, and left, and Greg said something about his brother."

"You said, more than once? What happened the next time?" Rudi was leaning forward, his eyes intent on her face, her every expression. She wondered anxiously if she were betraying some fact about Greg that would hurt him. She never wanted to hurt Greg. She worried again about where he was, if he might be a prisoner also.

"I had stayed late at the gallery, an artist had come who wanted a loan, and Greg must okay those. Well, Greg and this man he called his brother came in. And they had both been drinking."

"When was this?" he asked sharply.

"Just before we left on the trip. It was the day before, because the artist wanted badly to have some money before we left." She kept frowning, trying to remember the details. "Oh—let me see. It was half-dark in the gallery, the artist had bad eyesight, and wanted to save his vision. He was an older man. Greg and his brother came in, and they jumped when they realized we were there, and the brother cursed. Then Greg apologized to me, and said something about how badly his brother had been treated. In the war, and after."

"Did he say his name then? Did he introduce you?"

"No. The brother went into another room. Greg got some money for the artist. He is really very good with them, very kind and—he understands artists and tries to help them."

His quizzing was interrupted by a gentle knock on the door. Rudi let her go, and got up, went to the door and unlocked it. His valet Lothar came in wheeling a large table covered with drawings, paintings, and a bewildering variety of art. Caroline stared as the two men drew up the table to the sofa where she sat.

Rudi dismissed Lothar with a nod, and the valet disappeared. She noticed that Rudi had locked the door. Lothar went on into the room beyond the bedroom.

"I want you to see some of the Dornstein treasures, Caroline," said Rudi. He sat down beside her, and picked up a statuette. She had never seen it before. "How do you like it?" He put it into her hands.

"Oh, it is lovely, the carving—beautiful."

"And this one?" He held her another one. She gazed at it in bewilderment, her face mirroring her surprise.

"But it is—it is the same—I mean—"

"Identical." He told her grimly. "One is real, one is a fake. Which one is the fake, Caroline?"

She gazed from one to the other, shook her head. She turned around and around in her hands first one and then the other little Madonna figure, and shook her head again. "I don't know," she said meekly.

"Oh, come now. You have studied art in school and in college. You have artist friends, you have looked at good art. There are sure signs to tell the real from the imitation. Which is the real Madonna, the fourteenth century one?"

She set down the statuettes on the tray, carefully, her mouth compressed. "I told you I don't know," she said quietly.

He showed her a drawing, then another just like it, asked her coldly which was the real one. She peered at them, guessed tentativly that the older-looking on was real. He laid them down without commenting. He showed her more drawings, several statuettes, a triptych which really puzzled her. He did not show her a second one of that.

"Is this one real?" he asked.

She turned it round and round. She felt flushed and upset. She was bewildered by his cold manner, his questioning. What did he expect of her? She was no expert. She tried to tell him so. "I am no expert, Rudi. I just work for an expert. I am trying to learn, but I have just started and have many years of training to go through. This takes specialists—"

"Just tell me your opinion. Look at it, think about the aging of wood and paints, and tell me if this one is real."

She sighed deeply, turned the triptych around again. The little panels of three pictures were deftly done, in gleaming gold and ruby and blue and green. There were some cracks in the wood, the back was a little scarred. "All right, I will guess it is real," she said finally.

"Good. And this one?" He handed her one after another. She finally got tired of the game, and rather shortly gave her guesses, reckless of whether they might be right, or if her ignorance might be showing. She was ignorant.

He finally stopped. "Mother would like to talk to you this afternoon. Will you have coffee with her at four?"

She agreed eagerly. His mother did not seem deceitful, and Caroline would welcome the opportunity to question her. Rudi ate lunch with Caroline, then disappeared to his work, and she sat in the window seat, thankful she had not been drugged again. She wanted to enjoy the gardens below, and she wished she could go down and roam through them. She glimpsed the madman later in the afternoon, and guessed that the gardens were his safe retreat, that they let him play there because he could not get away and disturb anyone.

She watched the madman compassionately. He capered about, played with the water in the fountain as though he were reliving his childhood. A butterfly caught his attention, he chased it, caught it, held it on his finger, then let it go with a smile, tossing it up into the air to catch the wind, watching it flutter lazily away.

Trudi showed the countess in. She came in a flutter of white skirts, holding out her hands to Caroline.

"Oh, my dear new daughter," she exclaimed, in her husky musical voice. "How naughty of Rudi not to let me see you until now! We must have a good talk." And she drew her down beside her on the sofa.

The velvety black eyes, so like Rudi's, watched her steadily as they spoke. The white dress set off her still-dark hair, her olive skin, her still youthful figure.

"Will you tell me, please, why I am being kept here?" Caroline began impulsively. "Oh, please tell me, why does he keep me here? I know nothing about art—"

"Oh, darling, it is because he is selfish and wants to keep you to himself! I have told him so. But let us visit and become acquainted! Tell me about yourself." And she changed the subject so definitely that Caroline realized she had orders not to talk about Rudi, and his motives.

Rudi's mother was kind. She drew Caroline out and she found herself telling the countess about her early life.

"Mother and I never dreamed—she never did know— that Father was deeply in debt, that all the money was in the electronics business. He let us buy whatever we wanted. We had a lovely house, and a swimming pool in back. And I had a horse to ride at a nearby stable. I dearly loved my horse Chester. He was a deep chestnut color. Oh, I miss him."

Theresa von Dornstein was extremely pleased at her mention of horses, and began again to tell of some experiences of her own. They chatted away, and Trudi brought in coffee and cakes. The countess did not notice the locking and unlocking of the doors, or pretended not to.

The countess asked her gently about her mother, drew her out to talk about her schooling, the friends she had made. Caroline talked at length about Denise Hartman and what a strong influence she had had on her.

"She was only a year older than I, but so much more experienced! She had worked a year on her own before she came to college. She taught me the techniques I needed in drawing—so much more so than my teachers. But of course, she was so much better than I. And she would *order* me to read certain books," Caroline laughed softly at the memory. "When I knew I was coming to Europe, I wrote to Denise and told her. And of course she sent back a list of books I must read! In one month!"

"You only knew a month ahead of time you were coming? That's too bad," the countess sympathized.

"Yes, well, Greg never knows ahead of time what art he might acquire, he told me that. When he had collected many of the Dornstein items—I mean, ones he thought might be Dornstein—he decided to come and personally check their identification. That's the way he works."

"And is this your first trip to Europe?"

Caroline nodded. "The first on my own. I came with my parents once years ago, but I was so young it really didn't mean much to me. Father was trying to make some contacts with foreign firms to export—but it didn't work out, I found out much later."

"And this friend Denise Hartman—does her work resemble our old works, or does she paint in the modern vein?"

"Oh, very, very modern! Here, let me show you!" Caroline jumped up and got a pad of white paper. She tried earnestly to draw a sample design. "Oh, I can't do it well, but she would put red lines here, and purple ones here, and work them about with her fingertips until they blended, you see. I'm not good at drawing, the way she is," she apologized. "I wish you could see her work!"

"I should love to sometime, but I do not go to Vienna. Perhaps she would come here and visit you, and bring some of her work." And her face turned sad at the thought of Vienna, so that Caroline impulsively hugged her.

"I am sorry at all the things—those horrible things—that happened to you and yours," she said softly.

Tears filled the eyes of the countess, and she caught Caroline to her and pressed her cheek to hers. "You are a dear one, and I am glad that my Rudi married you," she said, in a choked voice.

They talked on and on, very comfortably, that afternoon, until the room turned dark and Trudi turned on the lights.

By the time the countess left, visibly reluctant to do so, Caroline felt she did indeed have a dear friend in her new mother-in-law. Surely the countess would not act this way as part of a game, she thought wistfully. She did indeed seem to love her and want Caroline to love her in return.

"I will come again very soon. But Rudi shall not be allowed to keep you to himself for long! I am determined on that. Our friends will want to come to know you, and he must bring you down to dinner soon," said the countess cheerfully as she took her departure with a sweep of her full white skirts.

Before she left, she caught Caroline in her arms, hugged her, kissed her cheeks and her lips gently. "You must look on me as your mother now," she said softly.

"Oh—I want to—so much," Caroline whispered, and pressed her cheek shyly to that of the older woman. She felt much better when she was finally alone, and her thoughts were less morbid as she waited for Rudi to return.

Chapter II

The next morning, Caroline again sat in the window seat, which was becoming her favorite place in the suite of apartments. From it, she could glimpse something of the life of the castle.

Sometimes the madman came out, and danced in the sunlight, and tossed water from the fountains like a small boy, absorbed in his thoughtless play. Sometimes the scarred guard, Kurt, leaned against a wall, or strolled near the cliffs, seemingly casually, but careful that his charge did not go too near the cliffs.

Sometimes maids would come out and hang a few pieces of kitchen laundry in the sunshine. Or a gardener would putter about among the roses and the pansy beds, or clip a few bushes.

Once she saw Rudi strolling there, his head bent in thought. He walked around for half an hour, pausing sometimes to gaze out over the valley and hills beyond. She almost held her breath, watching him, wondering what he was thinking.

Last night, she had had dinner with Rudi, lingering long over the light white wine and the coffee. Afterwards, she had soon felt drowsy, and had felt some panic and fear as she realized she had been drugged again. The dosage seemed lighter, but her mind was still slightly blurry.

Rudi had slept with her, but had not made love to her. She had been conscious of him whenever she wakened from her restless sleep and her dreaming. She kept dreaming of the war, of its terrors, of men with scarred faces, torments in barren-grounded concentration camps. Every picture she had ever seen of those gaunt men staring from behind barbed wire returned to haunt her sleep. Talking to Rudi and his mother about the war had brought it on, she thought. And thinking of the madman, Julius Mayer, and of scarred Kurt, who had undergone such horrors and lived—if you could call it living, Caroline thought with a shudder.

Trudi had put the pink linen on her today. Caroline did not care what she wore. Her mind was blurred again, and she realized she had received more of the drug at breakfast. Now she sat, her forehead against the warm window glass, and looked outside, and wished she could think clearly.

There was a knock at the door. Caroline jumped up nervously. Trudi went to the door, opened it to a man dressed in servant's livery. She began to scold him in German, pointing to several electric outlets.

The man nodded several times impatiently, and finally squatted down to look at the outlets and began to work, taking tools from the kit bag he had brought with him. Caroline's attention returned to the garden. She was stiting idly with her cheek against the window, when something white dropped into her lap.

She jerked, and glanced up. The repair man winked at her, gravely, put his hand to his lips, squatted down nearby to inspect an outlet near her. She saw Trudi swish past into the bedroom. The outer door had been locked again. She put her hand over the white enevlope in her lap, finally brushed it up under her sweater, her heart thumping.

When the repairman moved away, and Trudi was working in the bedroom, Caroline drew out the envelope, opened it furtively, and read the letter inside. It was in Greg's handwriting.

"My God, Caroline," it read. "Where are you? What are you doing? I am going crazy. We have to get out of here, everyone in this damned castle is insane! I am watched every minute. Everyone pretends you have returned to Vienna, and I know damn well it isn't so.

"This man agreed to carry a message to you, so I know you are somewhere in the castle. I paid him well. You can trust him. Try to get a note to me, or better yet meet me out near the garages. I'll steal a car and get us away if I have to. To hell with the art stuff—we have got to save ourselves. I'll wait for you, today or tonight. Come when you can. I'll take care of you, baby, don't worry. Love, Greg."

By the time she had finished the note, she was in a panic. Greg was still alive, but he was in grave danger, and so was she. What if everyone was insane? The madman was acknowledged to be. What if Rudi was also? Even his dear mother? The servants had been loyal for hundreds of generations to the Dornsteins. They would do whatever Rudi asked. And their friends would not care.

Trudi came back into the room. Caroline slipped the note into her sweater, stared out with tear-filled eyes at the garden. She was a prisoner. What could she do?

The man lingered, glanced a couple of times at Caroline. She did not dare move to write a note or send it. The man finally fixed the outlets—there was probably nothing wrong with them but a short, she guessed. He left. Trudi locked up behind him.

Caroline yawned again and again, behind her hand, then more obviously when Trudi did not seem to notice. She finally stood up casually, stretched, then said to Trudi, "I believe I shall lay down for a while," and she went into the bedroom. Trudi wanted her to change to a robe, Caroline shook her head. She slipped out of her shoes, lay down and put her head on the pillow.

Trudi covered her with a light blanket and tiptoed out. Caroline waited until everything was quiet, then silently rose again. There was another way out of the bedroom.

She put on her shoes, took her sweater and handbag, and tried the handle of the door to the next room. Her heart was beating so hard it hurt her. But she had to get out, she had to.

Her mind was not clear, it was fuzzy. She wished she could think. All she could do was feel, and now she felt blind panic, a fear of Rudi and everyone around her. She must get out and find Greg somehow. They had to get away. She was being drugged. He was in danger of his life.

The door opened, she peered inside, was relieved to see it was a small dressing room, equipped with wardrobe, mirror, couch. She tiptoed through it, opened the next door very carefully, and peeped inside.

There was another bedroom, as big as the other. She had thought the other was Rudi's, but now it seemed it must be her own, for this bedroom was furnished in a heavier, more masculine, style. Another huge bed, with a straight canopy of green silk. Big comfortable chairs. A large dresser and full-length mirror. Two wardrobes. A brown furry rug, perhaps a bearskin, lay on the floor near the right side of the bed.

She finally tiptoed through this bedroom also. Her thoughts absorbed by the huge room, she carelessly opened the next door and walked through it. She had thought, in her blurry mind, that she would be coming out into a hall-way.

Instead she blundered into a study. A study done in brown, green and gold. A mahogany desk behind which sat—Rudi. Rudi in shirt sleeves, bent over his desk, absorbed but alert. For he lifted his head instantly, as she walked in.

He stood up at once. "Ah, Caroline. Come in, my dear. But you are in. How may I serve you?"

She swallowed, her throat quite dry. What could she say? She could not think. "I was—I was—"

He came over to her, his eyes fixed on hers relentlessly. She shrank back, but he took her hand lightly, laid her handbag on a chair, and drew her over to the desk.

"Were you looking for me, my dear? Or for the way outside?" His tone was light, mocking, she thought.

"Oh—for—for you," she stammered, coloring. She was lying, and she was aware that he knew it.

"How nice of you." He paused, looked down at her speculatively. "But sometime you might wish to go outside. Let me show you the way!" He led her over to a side door, opened it. Outside was an iron staircase, with a light railing. It wound round and round, down into the garden a floor below. "You see? This way leads to the gardens. They are completely walled in, so you will be safe—so long as you do not go near the cliff, of course." His tone was dry and significant, she decided.

"It looks—lovely there. The view is what I see from my windows," she said shyly. "Perhaps I should walk there for a time today." And she moved to escape his hand.

"Not today, my dearest," he said, and drew her back inside, and shut the door. "You see, Uncle Julius is not very well today. He and Kurt are out there, because the garden soothes him. You would not be safe with him, I think."

She shivered. "No—I suppose not," she whispered. Greg's words returned to her, that everyone in the castle was insane. Oh, God, she thought, in despair. Everyone was indeed insane, and she was lost.

She stood with her head bent, Rudi's hand holding hers. She felt as trapped as a small animal, unable to move, fascinated by the trap, shuddering in its grip.

"Let me show you my work, then you shall tell me why you wanted to see me," he said, and drew her back to the desk. She looked down blankly, frantically searching for an excuse to present him. He indicated a large chart, it looked like a map.

"What is that?" she asked, touching the chart curiously.

"A map of the estate. You see, I must direct the work of the whole area. Most of the village is in the castle employ, and they farm the lands over here." He touched several areas. "These have been plowed, and are now being seeded. These meadows are pastures for cattle. Two men are ill, of a fever, and I must assign others to their jobs, while I obtain a doctor to see to them. Over here are some forest areas. Some were burned out many years ago. Look at this."

He moved the chart aside, took out a huge photograph which he spread out in its place.

"This is an aerial view taken a year ago. It covers much of Dornstein, from the border of Hungary to the village. This is how the burnt-out areas looked at the time. We decided to replant. And this is the view taken a few weeks ago." He spread another huge photograph beside it. Now his face was absorbed and serious. He was genuinely interested in his topic, as she leaned beside him and studied the photographs. He pointed out the places they had replanted with trees and shrubbery, fields lying fallow, other fields being plowed.

"Oh, I can see the difference already!" Her forefinger pointed to one photograph, then the other. "See—there—

how much richer it looks! It's marvelous. I should like to
see the new growth!"

He was gazing down at her as she looked at the photographs. She felt his hand touch her shoulder. "So you
shall, my dear. I shall show you everything—eventually. I
am pleased you take such an interest in Dornstein. You
will not want to wander away from our home, then." His
tone seemed drily mocking to her. She stiffened, and
dropped her hands, placing them behind her back, clasping
them together nervously. His hand was heavy on her
shoulder.

"Yes. Wander away," she repeated stupidly. "Of
course—not—Rudi."

"Good. Winifred was always talking about going off skiing, going around the world, buying a yacht to see the
Mediterranean ports. I thought she would probably never
take an interest in Dornstein. Now, you are quite different,
I saw that from the first."

She dared not meet his gaze. She had thought he was
mocking her for planning to run away from him. Winifred? She seemed a light year removed from this quiet
study, with its maps and charts, ancestors' portraits on the
walls, and the framed ancient map of the castle, with neat
little plots all about it.

"I am glad—I am different—from Winifred," she
managed to say scornfully. "She thought of nothing—but
pleasure—at least, I felt so."

"You felt correctly. She thinks of nothing but pleasure.
So did her parents, I believe. That is why they were Nazis,
for lack of the will to be anything else. I despise cowards
and weaklings." And now his voice rang true.

"I was talking to your mother about that," she began, to
end rather breathlessly. He was slowly drawing her to him.
"We—we agreed it is better—to die—than to live knowing
one had betrayed—"

She looked up at him wistfully. Did he understand she
could not, would not say anything that might unwittingly
betray Greg into his power? She did not know what he
wanted from her, he bewildered her. But she felt, somehow, that it was connected with Greg and the art, and
Rudi's desire to obtain it.

"My mother is very fond of you. I am glad," he said.
He lifted her chin with his fingers. His eyes were like
burning coals, like a panther's eyes, like a fire that might

burn or warm—she did not know which. "She did not approve of Winifred, nor of other young women I brought to her. Is it foolish of a son to think his mother knows women so well, that the one of whom she approves must be his choice? It was so with me, for she loved you at once. And I—I had begun to love you from the first moment I saw you, your hair blowing, that white coat and purple scarf setting off your lovely face, like an angel blowing down the street to the café—I could not believe you were the one I was to meet. I was thinking—how can I meet that lovely girl? How can I forget my appointment, and manage to meet her? And then—" And his lips came down on hers hungrily.

She could not think clearly, yet she was full of wonder. He had loved her at once? He had admired her, desired her, thought of her even as he talked so seriously to Greg? Yes, he had kept looking at her, Greg had remarked about it. Yet he had been so cold, so scornful—

The art. She felt cold again. Was he deceiving her once more? Was he lying to her? Was he charming her, to get some information from her that she did not even know she had?

What was he doing? What did he want from her? His arms were around her, holding her against him. She felt his heat through the thin white shirt, as he molded her against him. His lips were burning on hers.

"I am glad—" he whispered, mockingly, "that you came to look for me—I do not want to work, Caroline—Caroline—oh, you are so lovely—" And he picked her up and carried her through the open door to the bedroom beyond.

She lay passively in his arms as he carried her. She told herself she could not fight him because of the drug. But what if it was not just the drug?

What if she wanted him as much as he wanted her? She felt hot and weak, trembling with emotion, as he laid her on the bed, and took her in his arms again. He was pressing his mouth to her throat, hurriedly unfastening her dress to the waist, slipping his hand inside to find and cup her breast under the thin slip.

"Rudi—oh," she whispered, turning her head blindly on the thick pillows. "Rudi—oh—oh—" His hand was so knowing, as it moved down her opened dress. He was in a hurry this time, she knew that. His other hand ripped impatiently at her soft silky underclothes, until he had bared her.

Then he was moving on her, trying to slow down, trying to wait for her. But her body was already hot, and she felt so strange, so marvelous, that she did not want to think. She did not care about thinking.

She put her arms around his neck, held him to her breast, and he whispered wild words to her in German and in English, broken words, soft begging, pleading, demanding words. She hugged him more tightly, her cheek against his hair, which was so soft and crisp, so curly and black and fragrant.

They came together in a soft crash of flesh and heat and liquid desire, panting, holding, breaths catching and gasping. It was not like the first, not like the second time. It was different, wordless now, all need and satisfying.

He came high up into her, and she held him tightly, her eyes shut, feeling only, not thinking, feeling his hands on her, their bodies tightly clasped together, legs together, arms, bellies, thighs, breasts, lips.

She gloried in the sensations he was wakening in her. She had never felt like this in her life, so lost, so marvelously lost in another person. So completely one, so that she wanted never to move again.

He lay quietly beside her when it was over. When he stirred, he whispered to her, his voice mischievous, "I am so glad you came looking for me, darling. *Was this what you wanted?*"

Chapter 12

Caroline knew that Rudi gave her a heavier dose of drugs that night, probably with her coffee. She felt languid, dizzy, so dizzy that she fell asleep on the couch after dinner, and he carried her to her bedroom.

Trudi undressed her and put her to bed. She knew only vaguely that Rudi was there, murmuring to Trudi. He kissed Caroline's lips gently before he left.

Were they afraid she would succeed in running away? Rudi had not been deceived about her presence in his study. He knew she had been looking for a way out. He was a very clever man, with an uncanny way of reading her mind.

Yet—yet she admitted to herself that she loved him. She had only to think of him, to hear his name, and a wave of violent emotion would sweep through her. She thought—a crazy infatuation. Once away from him, safely back in New York, she could forget him again.

Forget? The way he held her, caressed her, whispered to her, the wild things he said, the way his hands moved over her, the way he took her? Could she ever wipe that out of her mind, ever cease to feel a thrill of desire at the very thought of him?

114

She slept late the next morning, awakening to feel languid, arms and body heavy. She stretched, yawned, felt no desire to get up, though the pretty antique gold clock near her bed said it was past eleven.

Trudi came in quietly, smiled to see her awake. She drew her bath, then helped Caroline into a new blue dress she had not seen before. She frowned down at it, in wonder. She started to ask Trudi where it came from, this pretty, soft blue confection with its white lace collar and cuffs. But Trudi was busily trying to tell her something about breakfast.

She brushed Caroline's hair to shining order, then fastened a matching blue ribbon about it, to hold it up a little from her shoulders. Caroline went into the living room to wait for breakfast.

She curled up on the couch, thoughtfully. What a different life this was from the hurry and bustle of her days and nights in New York! By twelve, she would have worked almost four hours, for Greg started early and ended late. She would be dashing out for a sandwich, bringing it back to have with coffee at her desk, while Greg lunched with a wealthy patron or a poor artist, trying to get the two of them together and narrow the wide gulf between them.

Greg. She had almost forgotten him again! How could she? He was probably worried sick about her, if he was not in even deeper trouble than she was. What was Rudi doing to him?

As though her thoughts had summoned him, Rudi came in quietly through the bedroom. She glanced up, and to her embarrassment felt color flooding into her cheeks. She had not seen him since last evening when she—

"Good morning, darling." He bent and kissed her cheek lightly, looked closely at her eyes. "How are you this morning? Rested?"

"Yes, thank you." The drug left her weak and quiet, but otherwise she felt well. "Rudi—please don't give me any more drugs," she said impulsively. "They make me feel so—so awful, so strange."

He touched her pulse in her wrist, lightly, his mouth losing its smile, his face curiously hard. "You must let me be the judge of what is best for you, Caroline. Now will you have breakfast or lunch?"

She looked at him mutinously. He shrugged. "I have ordered breakfast for you, lunch for me. But no drugs, for I have something to ask you, Caroline. Something to show you."

"What is it?" She felt apprehension again. His tone was so cold, so impersonal once more. She sighed. She did not know whether she wanted him to be more loving and kind—or to be cold and hard so she could stop loving him so crazily.

"After lunch," he said. He touched the white lace collar lightly with his finger. "The dress suits you, I thought it would."

"Where—did it come from?" she asked, looking down soberly at herself. At any other time, she would have felt pleasure in such a pretty new dress.

"From Vienna. I sent for several new dresses for you." He seated himself in a chair near her place on the couch, and she felt suddenly unreasonably disappointed that he was so far away. What was wrong with her? Had he bewitched her? Was she hypnotized as well as drugged? "There is a lavender one I believe will match your eyes. They are—" He leaned forward, looked keenly again into her eyes. "No—they are violet, a deep violet this morning. The shade will be too pale." He half-smiled, as though looking at her gave him pleasure, then he looked away again.

A servant wheeled in a large table. He served them silently, omelette and bacon for Caroline, omelette and a veal cutlet for Rudi. She seemed to have lost her appetite, and contented herself with breaking open a hot biscuit, buttering it, eating it slowly with her creamy rich coffee. She thought he would not notice she was toying with her food.

He did not look up from his cutlet and white asparagus. "Eat, Caroline, you eat too little. You are much too thin, now."

She started nervously, began to protest. "It is the fashion to be thin. And I am not very hungry—"

"In America, perhaps. I want you to be healthy. Try the omelette." When she did not lift her fork, he leaned forward, took the fork, broke off a little of the omeletet and put it to her mouth. She grimaced at him daringly, but took it. It was very good, fluffy and light, and seasoned just right, with a few mushrooms in it.

"It is strange how fashions change," she said, to make conversation.

"Yes. Strange how lives change," he added absently. "Do you know—during the war how little food there was? We ate what we had, and were glad for it. And I think now I was never so hungry and so satisfied with my food, as when I was a child, running from one place to another. Banquets nauseate me now, when I see the wasted food, the plates sent back to the kitchen almost untouched."

He went on talking about the war, as they ate, almost as though he were compelled to talk about it. He told her about the resistance movement, the student movement, the rebellion within the Austrian army. He told her about his father and his uncle, the parts they had played, how they were captured.

"They were betrayed, Caroline. The old hates run deep here. Some old scores were paid off, yes, and new ones added to be settled later," and there was a white pinched line on either side of his aristocratic nose.

"And of all qualities, you hate most disloyalty—and cowardice," she said, quietly.

He looked over at her, studying her. She met his gaze for a full minute before she looked down again. Did he think she would betray Greg? He would never betray anyone, her proud husband. He would die first.

"Yes, yes, of course," he said, as though his mind was elsewhere. "Yes. Did you know about these movements? Had you heard of them?"

"I have read about them in books," she said. "But the facts seemed abstract to me, until you told me about your relatives and friends."

"Always. Yes, in the books—cold statistics." He sipped his coffee, frowning. "Next to lives and torture, it was minor when the art treasures were confiscated or stolen. But we felt it deeply, we who had lived with these treasures and preserved them over many years."

She stiffened. Ah, now he was getting to the part that concerned her. "I would imagine so. You ought to be very grateful to Greg Alpert for helping restore them to you," she told him with chilly emphasis.

"Grateful? Yes, yes." He touched a silver bell near him, and she started at the sudden chiming sound. The servant gathered up the napkins to take the table away.

She waited. A few moments later, Lothar wheeled in another table. Caroline braced herself for another strange inquisition, for on the table were more art objects, paintings, drawings, wood carvings, along with stacks of aged books of records.

"More coffee? No, then you may take it away," he added to the servant. Rudi sat before the table, lifted one book, and placed in before Caroline. She waited, her hands in her lap, for whatever trial might be before her.

He indicated several pages. She leaned forward and looked at them curiously, in spite of her apprehension.

"These are records of the Dornstein art treasures," he said. "These pages show what was added in the seventeenth century. The earlier records are all the treasures of the sixteenth, when an inventory was taken. Later treasures were catalogued immediately, when they were acquired."

She studied the ancient writing, frowned over it. It was in the old German script, and she had trouble even deciphering the letters in the thick black ink, much less translating it. Rudi translated for her, patiently, reading entries aloud, as his finger followed the lines.

"That item is this triptych here," he said, then, and picked up the small gilded three-panel piece. She held it in her hands, studying it, as he read the description again. "You see, it matches, even to the small flaw where the robe of the angel was scratched and the gold paint flecked off." He showed it to her.

"Oh, yes, I see it now. But it is such a tiny thing!"

"Small, but significant. It helps identify the object. We had hidden it in the cellars before we fled," he said, casually. He laid it aside, handed her a drawing. "These papers became slightly musty in the years they were in the cellars. I remember Mother laying them out on the grass like laundry—on sunny days, to dry them out."

He showed her more objects, then put a statute in her hands. He read her the description.

"Do you like it?" he asked.

"Oh, yes, it is fine, I think," she said, dubiously. He put another in her hand.

She gasped. "But they are just alike!" she cried.

"Not just alike. One is the original, one a fake. Listen once again." And he read the description from the record, translating the German for her. She puzzled over the objects. She didn't care much for the statuette, it was one of those she secretly called "bloody Christs," with realistic wounds and dripping blood painted red. She could not see the difference, no matter how she looked.

"They look alike to me," she said. "Well—maybe this is the real one. There is a crack here," she added eagerly.

He smiled, rather strangely. "Was there a crack in the descriptive paragraph about it?"

"Well—no, but it could have been damaged later, couldn't it?"

He shook his head. "That information would have been added to the record. No, this one is the real, the one with the crack is a fake. The error was made by a hasty forger, who had read a description of another statuette, and got the two confused."

"Oh, I see," she said, in a small voice. He showed her others, then asked her which was real and which was fake. She was wrong about half the time. The color came and went in her cheeks. She felt quite embarrassed about her mistakes.

Rudi grew strangely more cheerful as the afternoon went on. She supposed he enjoyed her stupidity, and finally said so resentfully. "You like to think me a fool!" she cried out, after a particularly bad mistake on her part. Her eyes flashed with rage. "You should know I don't have the experience! I studied art in school, I can draw and paint a little, that doesn't mean I am an expert!"

He only laughed. "No, my dear, I don't think you a fool. You are a very intelligent woman, that was the trouble," he said, while she stared at him in bewilderment.

"Trouble? To be intelligent? I don't understand you, Rudi!" she burst out. "Are you one of those men who like to think women are better off stupid? If so, you had better let me go at once! Marry a moron, if that pleases you! And let me go back to New York, where intelligence doesn't seem to be such a drawback for a female!"

"Oh, yes, I have heard of Women's Liberation," he said, and chuckled again. "But it does not displease me that you are intelligent, Caroline. On the contrary, you will be an asset to me, and to the Dornstein family, I am confident."

She was so puzzled that she stared at him in bewilderment and with some resentment. He was so contradictory! And why did he imply that she would live here as his wife to continue the Dornstein family line? She brushed back her hair nervously, aware he was gazing at her.

"Yes, I think we know each other better now, do we

not?" he said, gently, and touched her hair with a lingering hand. "Do not worry, we shall become even better acquainted as the days and weeks and years continue. And
now, please consider this small painting."

Disturbed, her mind in tumult with puzzlement, she still
could thrill at the beauty of the painting he handed to her.
"Oh—Rudi—how exquisite! Who is she?"

"My great-grandmother, on my mother's side. A
Magyar princess. Look at her fiery black eyes. Of whom
does she remind you?"

Caroline smiled down at the handsome face, the flashing
eyes, the beauty of the girl in her red and white satin and
lace, the jewels flashing in her black curly hair. "Of you,"
she said, absently.

He chuckled again. "Yes, but I meant—of my mother,
surely?"

"Oh, yes, of course. But you and your mother are much
alike." She could not take her eyes from the small
painting, about nine by twelve inches, on a wooden panel,
with the most delicate brush strokes imaginable, with the
clear reds and whites, blacks and greens and blues, like a
miniature.

"It will be interesting to see what coloring our children
have," he said. "With your blonde hair and violet eyes,
and my black hair and eyes—whom shall they resemble? I
wonder if we shall have a small girl with blonde hair and
black eyes, or a black-haired boy with purple eyes?"

Now she did blush violently. He took the painting from
her suddenly nerveless hands. He was really taking a great
deal for granted! Had the marriage been a real one after
all, or was he planning the deception so elaborately that
she would be fooled?

"You do not answer me," he said, with a smile. "Except
that your lovely face is quite flushed." And he leaned forward and kissed her warm cheek.

She jumped up. "I think—I think I have seen enough
paintings—and a-art for one—d-day," she stammered. "I
don't know why you show me all this, what your purpose
is."

"Why, you are a Dornstein now," he said, smoothly, as
he rose and took her hands in his. "You must become acquainted with all the treasures and learn to know them.
And Mother will later acquaint you with the household
duties, the managing of the estate, the resources and re-

sponsibilities you will have. I have only just begun to inform you of one fraction of the Dornstein possessions. Shall you enjoy them all, I wonder? Did you know we have a hundred or more horses, of the finest breeding? Do you like to ride?

"But of course you enjoy riding. And you are well-coordinated—you will later learn to ski—to sail. You swim now, I am sure. And you dance—like a dream—"

And he began to hum, a Strauss waltz, his eyes flashing down into hers. Unexpectedly, he put his arm about her waist, and drew her with him into a whirling dance, making them fly about the room. He danced as well as he moved, as indistinctively rhythmic as a gypsy, she thought, and he made her move as lightly and beautifully as he did.

His arm was tightly about her, his hand clasped hers, and pulled her to him as they danced around and around and around, until she was dizzy.

"Oh—Rudi—I am—dizzy," she panted, leaning back against his arm.

"Then close your eyes, little one!" And he only laughed, when she closed her eyes, and he whirled her about madly. "Ah, I am happy—dum, de-dum—dum, de-dum—I love that song, the waltz is a happy melody—"

He whirled her around and around, and ended by catching her close with both arms. His kisses fell on her face, on her lips, on her eyelids, as she tried to catch her breath.

She knew he was happy, gay and carefree for once, but she did not know why. She did not understand him at all. She had blundered, had answered stupidly, and he was pleased! Why?

Chapter 13

During the following two days, Caroline knew she was still being drugged. However, either she was developing a tolerance or was being given a lighter dosage. She did not feel so dizzy and sleepy as she had at first.

The countess came for tea one day. They had a long comfortable chat about many things. Rudi's mother seemed to enjoy speaking of the days when Rudi was a small boy. And Caroline was hungry for any scraps of information about him, clues to his character, to the enigma that was Rudi today.

The countess drew her out to speak also of her early life, and Caroline was able to relax and tell her whatever she wanted. The countess reminded her somewhat of Denise Hartman, full of wise advice and a little dictatorial about what she ought to think and do! Caroline hoped that if she was really Rudi's wife and would remain here that Rudi's mother and she would become good friends as well as relatives.

Rudi came in toward dusk. His mother greeted him affectionately, Caroline rather shyly. She had not seen him all day, and very little the day before. She had slept alone the night before. She did not know where Rudi had gone; he did not confide in her about his activities.

Rudi bent and kissed his mother's cheek, then bent to Caroline, studied her face swiftly. He lifted her chin with his finger, bent and kissed her lips.

"Did you enjoy today, my darling?" he asked, in a caressing voice.

The color swiftly flooded her cheeks. She was not used to having him speak to her in that wooing tone. "Yes, your mother came to tea," she said, then blushed again at her stupid response.

"I am pleased that you and Mother are not fighting constantly," said Rudi, laughter in his eyes, as he lounged in a chair near Caroline. "I dislike quarreling and bickering."

"No, Rudi, you prefer to have everything your own way," said his mother, tartly. "Caroline and I understand each other, do we not, love? But you, Rudi, you must ever have things as you choose, with no discussion!"

"Of course, Mother," he agreed, lazily, a gleam in his black eyes, a slight sardonic smile quirking the corner of his handsome mouth.

The countess frowned, she was not amused by this exchange. Caroline looked from one to the other, the two Magyars, the two passionate, highly volatile people she was just beginning to know. They puzzled her. This was about something important, she realized, but what the subject was she did not know.

The countess began to speak rapidly in German. Rudi lifted his hand suddenly, commandingly, as though to physically chop off her remarks. The mother compressed her mouth into a pout of disapproval, and changed what she was saying to English.

"Several dresses have arrived for you from Vienna, darling," she said to Caroline, and it was obvious that this was not what she had been saying so forcefully in German. "May I not see them soon? You look so lovely in that gown," and she leaned forward to touch the delicate fabric of a pale green silk dress, with purple violets embroidered in a scattered pattern on the hem and sleeves.

Caroline sat up straight, prepared to answer her request. Rudi shook his head. "No, Mother, in good time. You will see them as Caroline appears in them. Besides, I want to surprise Caroline. She has not seen them all yet," he added, with a little laugh at Caroline's surprised face.

"But Trudi put several into the closet, and I have worn a new one every day," she began.

"But there are others," he added, and laughed again, the lines of his face relaxing. "It is fun to dress you, you are like a pretty doll!"

"And stupid as a stuffed doll!" Caroline flashed quickly, and her eyes snapped. "That is what you think!"

His mother looked amazed. "Oh, no, surely not."

"Of course not," said Rudi, decidedly. "Quite the contrary. You have caused me some anxious moments, but it will all be worth it—I assure you, Mother!" he added sternly to his mother.

The woman sighed, shrugged. Caroline was more confused than ever. The countess got up to leave, saying she must return to the guests. "You will not keep her to yourself forever, Rudi!" she said to Rudi as they went to the door.

He said something rapidly, low, in German. She answered angrily, swiftly, and the exchange at the doorway took quite five minutes before the countess shrugged, turned and waved with a smile to Caroline, and left them.

Rudi came back, looking very thoughtful. "Did you understand the German?" he asked Caroline, casually. "Or is it still too much for you?"

"No, my vocabulary is still not very extensive, and when German is spoken quickly I do not catch the words at all," she said, thinking he was mocking her intelligence again.

"Later on, we will obtain a good tutor for you. I want you to speak German fluently. Well—" He sat down beside her and took her hand to play with in his. She looked down at their joined hands, as he toyed with her fingers. He closed his hand gently, enclosing all her hand in his, then opened it again, as though he were comparing the sizes.

Trudi came in as they sat silently, and paused abruptly on the threshhold. "Ah—excuse me!" And she started to whirl about and leave.

"No, no, come in, Trudi. I want my wife to wear the new blue dress tonight, the one I unpacked today. It is ready?"

"Oh, yes, sir!" And she beamed with pleasure. "And the other one, the—"

"Sh, sh, sh," he stopped her with a laugh and admonition. "That will be another surprise!"

She clapped her hand over her mouth, and her eyes laughed over the hand as she shared some secret with him.

Caroline shook her head slightly. He could be so kind, with lovely surprises, then turn about and speak so sarcastically, or question her so sharply about Greg and art. She simply did not understand it.

Trudi dressed her in the new dress. It was a short deep blue chiffon evening dress, with long full sleeves. There was also a pair of sapphire drop earrings and a matching bracelet which must have cost a fortune, she thought. She felt as though she were in costume, acting a part, without knowing what part she had been cast for.

She came out rather soberly to the living room, where Rudi waited. He had changed from his outdoor clothes to a gray velvet suit, white frilled shirt. He glanced at her keenly, said quietly, "Is something wrong, Caroline? You do not like the dress?"

She looked down and fluffed the skirt childishly, with pleasure. "Oh, no, it is quite the loveliest dress I have ever worn—and the jewelry—oh, Rudi, it is gorgeous. I am almost afraid to wear it."

He flicked the earrings lightly with his fingertip, to make them swing, and smiled down at her. His mouth was not hard tonight, but tender, his eyes softened.

"They are not quite so blue as your beautiful eyes." And he kissed her eyes shut, softly, before he released her.

They ate dinner, and she could not have said later what they ate. He kept looking at her, talking in that low, intimate, husky tone that turned her knees to water. It was not so much what he said, for he talked about his mother, the old days, the castle and the work he was doing. But the way he looked at her, as though he could eat her up, she thought, rather nervously. When he ran his hand casually down her chiffon-sleeved arm, a shiver went right through her, and he knew it, she could tell by his slow smile.

The servant brought their dessert, strawberries in thick rich cream, with coffee and more cream. She drank her coffee slowly, reluctant to end the meal, a little afraid of what might happen. She wondered if he would drug her heavily again. Now that the drugs were lighter she had started to worry again, and felt that with his keenness he could read her mind.

Lothar entered the room rather hastily, and spoke to his master in a strange dialect. It was not German, thought Caroline, or not the German she was used to. She could not understand it at all.

Rudi listened, frowned, nodded, spoke brusquely the same way. Then he turned to Caroline. "I am sorry, darling, I must leave for a little while. Wait here for me. I shall return soon."

And he left the room, locking it after him. She abruptly felt uneasy, thinking of the sudden coldness in his black eyes, the set lines of his face. What could have happened? Was it something to do with her—with Greg?

She got up to pace the room, clasping her hands tightly together. In the midst of her chaotic thoughts she heard music. She paused, then went to the windows, and peered down into the dark garden below.

She saw nothing, but on opening the casement she could hear the music more clearly. A single violin, played with an expert touch. An ancient song, then some fragments from Mendelssohn, then another song.

She was puzzled, intrigued. Who could be playing? And Rudi—Rudi was coming back soon, in what mood she could not know.

She acted on impulse. Rudi had left hastily, he might not have locked all the doors of the suite. He usually did not when he was with her.

She walked into her bedroom. Trudi had disappeared— discreetly, Caroline judged, with her mouth a little twisted. Rudi would be able to charm her if he choose. He could do anything he wanted with her already. He had made her fall in love with him, though she did not understand or trust him at all.

She went quietly through to the next room, then to Rudi's large bedroom. She walked hastily through the room, remembering—

She came out into his study, and hesitated. A lamp was burning on the desk. But no one was there. She went past the desk, to the side door he had opened. She tried it. It was not locked. She opened it cautiously, peered down into the garden, past the twisting steps.

She could see nothing, but the violin was playing, more

steadily and confidently now. She followed the sound, holding her chiffon skirt back from the railing, cautiously descending in her high-heeled silk shoes.

She followed the sound, as far as the fountain in the center of the garden. Then the sound stopped, abruptly, in the middle of a cascade of notes rippling—dropping into silence.

She glanced about her, puzzled. Had it been a record? A tape recorder perhaps? "Hello? Who was playing?" she asked, cautiously. She turned around slowly. "Who—oooohhhh!"

Directly behind her was the madman.

He was glaring at her, his black eyes fierce in the moonlight. His white hair was ruffled by the wind, his thin face twisted in fury. But in his hands were a violin and a bow.

She drew a deep steadying breath. She spoke very quietly, as Rudi had spoken.

"Was it you—playing the violin? How beautifully you play."

He was still glaring at her, standing where she could not escape from him, between her and the stairs. His mouth was working nervously.

"You—played—something by Mendelssohn," she said again. "Would you play it again? For me?"

"Uh—uh—Mendelssohn," he said. She had spoken slowly in German, and he replied in German. "You like him? He wrote so—sweetly."

"Yes, very sweetly. Will you play for me?"

He was staring at her, his eyes calming now. "I will play—a dance—for you," he said. "You are—so beautiful—and you are—wearing a dress—for dancing—"

He lifted the violin to his shoulder, bent his cheek to it, and began to play. The eyes still held hers suspiciously, watchfully, but he played exquisitely, holding the notes, making the tune dance under his fingers. She smiled involuntarily, happily, at the beauty of the tune.

When he had finished, she murmured, "Thank you. That was lovely."

"Who are you?" he asked.

She drew a deep breath. "I am Caroline. Rudi married me. You came to our wedding—in the chapel."

Would he remember? Or would he turn angry and

growl and try to attack her? She tried to appear calm, and clasped her hands slowly before her.

"You wore—a white dress. Theresa's—wedding dress, and the white veil, I remember."

"Yes. She let me wear her dress. I am the same size she was when she was married."

"Oh, Caroline, here you are, my darling." Rudi came up slowly to their side. The madman turned quickly, watchfully, keeping them both in view.

"Yes, he was playing a tune for me," she said. Rudi put his arm about her waist as he came to her. To her amazement, his arm was shaking.

"I heard him. Uncle Julius, you play as beautifully as ever. I remember when you played for our dancing. The ballroom of the castle was filled with light and beautiful ladies dancing as you played."

"Oh—yes—yes—" And the man began to smile, his eyes lighting up at the memory. "I remember—Betty wore a blue dress. Like—like Caroline's. Only it was long, to her ankles. And Theresa wore rose, do you remember her rose dress?"

"She would be lovely in rose," said Caroline quietly. Rudi was clasping her almost painfully tight. She had heard a catch in his voice, a slight quiver, that told her he was under an intense strain. He had been afraid of her.

They talked slowly about the past. Caroline was able to talk to Uncle Julius, he could talk to her, and he seemed to relax as they spoke. His eyes no longer glittered with suspicion.

As they talked, Kurt came up slowly, from the side so that Julius could see him and recognize him, and not be startled. Julius' eyes followed him quickly, registered him, and flicked away again.

Kurt came to them, stood listening as they spoke. They were again talking about music.

"What was the tune you played for me?" asked Caroline. "It was familiar, yet a little different—"

Julius lifted the violin, played a little snatch of it, then explained, "It is really a Hungarian folk tune. Now it is a popular song, but they have changed it. I play the way it was at first, when we danced in the gypsy camps, and watched the girls whirl about. Ah, I remember the scent of the pines . . ." His voice trailed off, he bent his head, as memories of the past seemed to flood him.

"It is time for bed," said Kurt finally, as he was silent. He nodded slowly.

He said goodnight to them, then seeming to remember, he lifted Caroline's hand in his, and put it to his lips in courtly fashion. "Good night—Caroline," he said.

"Good night, Uncle Julius," she said softly, smiling at him.

She and Rudi watched him go, the thin, erect man and the hulking scar-faced guard who was his close friend. Rudi's arm crushed her for a moment against him before he loosened his grip.

"Caroline, I was never so frightened—if you ever do that again! I was in torment—" His voice was husky. "What if something had happened—"

"I heard him playing the violin. Rudi, I could talk to him! I could."

"I know, I know, I heard you. It was marvelous. He can be reached, and your gentleness and sweetness—" His voice died. He pulled her to him, lifted her face for his kisses. "I am grateful—grateful, darling—oh, how did I get so lucky? That I found you—that I found you—after all these years, to find the lovely one, the girl of my dreams—" His voice was so husky she could scarcely understand the words he murmured in German.

They went back up the winding stairs to their rooms, slowly, his arm about her. In the dimness of his bedroom, he unfastened the blue chiffon dress, undressed her with caressing hands. He lifted her in his arms, held her high against his breast, kissing her with such gentleness and tenderness that she clasped her arms about his neck and relaxed in his embrace.

He laid her down on the bed, finally, and she waited while he stripped himself rapidly. This time she waited eagerly. She felt dizzy—but not with drugs. She was swept out of herself, full of an expectant hunger, a tremendous wonder, an eager waiting, for what would come.

And he made love to her so tenderly, so gently, that she finally cried with her response, turning her head back and forth on the pillow as the ecstasy swept through her again and again. His hands were so skilled, so marvelous in awakening her to the wonders of his love. His lips were warm on her flesh, searching out the sweet, intimate places to kiss. And his body, so hard and muscular against her tender curves.

She held him to her, with all her strength, and finally answered in words as he begged her. "Yes, yes, I love you—I love you—I love you—" she moaned, trembling. His lips crushed hers. And it was like the music singing through her blood, making her dance and quiver with pleasure, as he loved her passionately.

Chapter 14

Rudi gradually stopped giving her drugs. Caroline realized this as in the next few days her head seemed to clear, and she was not nearly so sleepy and dizzy.

She was still locked in the suite of rooms. However, the door to the stairway leading to the gardens was kept unlocked. She spent some time in the sunshine, dreaming, walking along the cobbled paths among the roses, pansies, phlox, stock, snapdragons.

Sometimes Uncle Julius was there. Kurt was always beside him, his eyes watchful. When Julius was calm, he would talk to Caroline a little, shyly. At other times he seemed restless, angry, and ran about the gardens wildly, as though trying to escape his own crazed thoughts.

Caroline was beginning to think she would be locked off from the world forever. She worried about Greg, wondered how he was, what Rudi might be doing to him. When she asked Rudi about Greg, he would cut her off sharply, frown, or refuse to answer. She knew that the situation was bad, and that it was urgent. But there seemed nothing she could do about it.

Then one evening she returned to her bedroom before dinner to be dressed by Trudi for dinner. She had not seen

Rudi since the previous evening, when he had been called away by Lothar as they were drinking coffee. He had not returned, though she had lain awake waiting for him.

On the green velvet chair near her lay a gorgeous new dress of white satin brocade sewn with pearls. Caroline exclaimed over it, touching the low-cut bodice, the puffed sleeves sewn with loops of pearls. Trudi was beaming with pleasure over the surprise.

The maid dressed her in the long gown, and produced a pair of white satin shoes. Then she proceeded to brush her hair back, and dress it with formal curls leaving Caroline's neck bare, and her ears showing.

It was like a bridal gown, she thought, as Trudi added a pearl necklace, the large emerald ring, and pearl earrings. Caroline stood up and Trudi adjusted the skirt deftly, so it stood out in a billow of white brocade.

Rudi entered from his bedroom. Caroline blinked at his splendor. He wore what looked like a uniform of forest green, decorated with shoulder cords of gold, with more gold on the sleeves. His shirt was white, with a frilled lace front and stand-up collar. He looked like a portrait of one of his ancestors, with his black curly hair brushed hard, his black eyes cold and determined.

He paused to look at Caroline, his gaze critical. "Yes— yes. That is right," he murmured.

Trudi babbled in German, "How beautiful she is, like a bride! Look how the dress becomes her—"

"Yes, I see it does. Like a bride yes. Come, Caroline," he said, and held out his arm to her formally. He did not praise her looks, or gaze at her with affection. He seemed absorbed in his own thoughts, frowning. She looked up at him wonderingly.

Just when she thought she was beginning to know him, he would surprise her with some new aspect of himself.

He led her into the sitting room, but they did not pause there. He went to the locked door with her, unlocked it, and led her out into the hallway. She was further surprised as they walked along the long corridor to the top of the stairway leading to the floor below. As she gazed down, she saw the crystal chandeliers ablaze with light, and white roses and ribbons twined along the railings of the staircase. They descended as the guests began to come out from the other rooms to gaze up at them.

She saw Rudi's mother first, radiant in a purple velvet

gown, her black curly hair covered with a tiara of diamonds and amethysts. Near her were the Hintereggers, formally gowned, with their tall blonde daughter in a white chiffon pants suit. Caroline caught Winifred's sulky, incredulous look as she stared up at her.

Baron von Ehrenberg was escorting Madame Zollner, and both beamed up at the couple as they came. Madame Zollner called out, "Ah, the lovely people, the beautiful people! Best wishes, congratulations, how lovely, how beautiful you are!"

Old Wolfgang Gruber was nodding his white head, his cheeks flushed with excitement as he hobbled from one of the drawing rooms to a place of honor near the bottom of the stairs. And then Caroline saw Greg slowly enter the hall, saw his face whiten, his eyes stricken with something like pain and incredulity as he gazed at Caroline dressed in white, like a bride.

"Greg," she said softly, almost to herself. Rudi's hand tightened cruelly on hers, and she winced. They reached the foot of the stairs, and the countess rustled up to them. She kissed Caroline's cheek, then Rudi's, then took a hand of each and turned to present them to her guests.

Caroline scarcely took in the flowery presentations, first in German and then in English, as the countess introduced her new daughter-in-law. She caught the words, "My pearl, my treasure, my new lovely daughter, the new countess—"

The woman meant *her*, Caroline. She stood frozen, wondering when someone would start to laugh and break up the masquerade. She was not truly married to Rudi, not to the Graf von Dornstein, heir of a family with a thousand-year lineage! It could not be true. Someone would now expose the joke, and she could leave—

Leave Rudi, leave those rooms upstairs, leave the castle, leave—leave the man she had reluctantly come to love.

As the speech ended she felt pain in her heart, pain and anger and despair. How could she endure their laughter, how could she stand this? And worst of all—to know that Rudi, the man she had come to love, could have played such a trick on her in order to obtain the family treasures for nothing. She could not but believe it was his purpose.

The countess ended her speech, wiped a few tears from her eyes, kissed Caroline gently on her cheek. Rudi began his answer, in an equally flowery but more formal way, thanking his mother and his guests for their welcome and best wishes.

When would it end? Rudi's speech concluded, and the elderly Wolfgang Gruber began a long reply. Somehow Rudi managed to sweep them all into one of the drawing rooms as the speech went on. They gathered about a long table set with a huge punch bowl and white wedding cake.

Someone handed Caroline a knife. Rudi's hand guided hers as she tried to cut it awkwardly. She managed to slice off a piece, and she and Rudi ate it.

A servant continued the cake cutting. Someone— Rudi—pressed a cup of champagne into her hand. She drank thirstily, her hand shaking from the strain. Someone drew Rudi away from her, it was Winifred Hinteregger.

"Rudi, how bad of you not to invite us to the wedding! And to hide your bride away for more than a week!" She was scolding him, in a cooing tone that did not disguise the strong dislike in her eyes as she glanced at Caroline. "I was never so shocked! I had no idea you went for Americans!" She lowered her voice, and spoke in German, but Caroline heard her clearly. She knew she was meant to hear this. Caroline turned away.

Greg caught her arm, drew her farther away. His face was strained under his light tan. His eyes were haunted. "Caroline. What happened? Tell me fast! God, these days have been horrible! What happened to you?"

She glanced around, saw they were a little apart from the other guests. She said, in a low tone, "I was married to—Rudi—in the chapel. A fake marriage. They are going through some sort of masquerade, I don't know why. What has been happening to you?"

He pressed his hand to his forehead. "God, this is a nightmare! I have been questioned over and over about the art. You would think I was a thief! They asked again and again where I got the stuff, who sold it to me, what channels it came through. I just refused to answer. I was locked in my room several times, treated like a prisoner! And I was told that you were locked up too, and then some vague story about your marrying that guy! What did he do to you?"

Caroline could not stop the swift blush that came to her cheeks. She stammered, "Oh, I—I married him, did what I was told, but I was worried about you. They asked me about the art as well. They showed me identical drawings, and asked me which was real and which was fake."

Greg glared down at her, his gray-green eyes frightened. "They did—what? Showed you identical pieces? Some I brought?"

"No—no, I don't think so." She was glad the subject had been changed from her marriage. Greg seemed really horrified now. "I think they were pieces from the Dornstein collection." She raised her eyes, as though impelled, and saw Rudi looking at her from over the heads of several persons near him. He gazed directly at her, and then a slight smile came to his lips. His eyes were black as two coals.

She caught her breath. Was there a threat in that gaze? He made no move to approach her, to break up the conversation. She turned slightly away, and continued her conversation with Greg.

Greg lowered his voice so much she could scarcely hear him. She leaned closer to hear. He caught her arm, murmured into her ear, "What did they ask you? What did *he* ask?"

"Oh—he asked about you, your connections in New York. Oh, and he asked if you had a brother."

Greg caught his breath audibly. "What did you say?" he asked harshly.

"I told him you did, but I couldn't remember his name," and she looked up at him anxiously, to find him shaking. "Greg! What is it? What's wrong?"

He shook himself slightly, finally answered in a low growl, "God, Caroline, you may have signed my brother's death warrant! He fought these Nazis! He was their prisoner for years! You may have put him in their hands again! They are all mad!"

She swayed with the shock. "Oh—no—Greg!" she whispered. "No, I would not do that—never—oh, I never knew—how could they get him—how—"

"They have their ways. Oh, they have long memories! And he fooled them, got away, rescued prisoners from them. God, Caroline, if they guess—if they find him—they will torture and murder him as they tried to do before!" He shook her arm a little.

"Oh, I never would—never—Greg, if I had known—"

"Promise me," he whispered rapidly, "you will tell nothing more about my brother! His life—and mine—are in your hands! They might try to hold me hostage. In fact they may be doing so right now! The art may have been a camouflage to get me here, a lure to get me in their trap. Then they will hold me, force my brother to come—if they know! Don't tell them another thing, promise me—promise me—"

Caroline had opened her lips to speak, horrified at Greg's convulsed face, when a cool drawl sounded at her shoulder. A grip of steel took her arm.

"What do you want my wife to promise you, Mr. Alpert?" Rudi loomed over them both, his face dark and ominous.

Greg muttered something and pushed away into the crowd. Rudi took Caroline's empty cup, and steered her in another direction. "More champagne, my dearest?" he said in the cool deadly way that made her shudder. "I must protest your showering your attentions on another man, my wife! You do belong to me, remember!"

She could not look into his eyes. He was insanely jealous and possessive, she thought. His grip hurt her. How much had he overheard before he had interrupted?

Would he, could he murder Greg and his brother? And herself? She did not doubt it. No one deceived or hurt the Dornsteins, he had told her, without bringing down the wrath and vengeance of the family.

She took the full cup he offered her, but her hand was shaking. He watched her a moment, then put his hand around hers to lift the cup to her lips. She drank again, and felt as dizzy as after the drugs. It was a strong punch, more champagne than fruit.

He said again, more quietly, "What did Mr. Alpert want you to promise him, Caroline?"

"I—I cannot—tell you," she defied him faintly.

"We will speak of this later," he said, with the steel ring in his voice once more. "Remember, you owe him nothing. And you belong to me now."

She flung back her head proudly, his words stinging. "I do not belong to anyone! I am myself, and I—"

He put his hand on her slight shoulder and pressed. The fingers bit into her flesh, and the words died on her lips. Yes, he was much stronger than she, she thought bitterly.

"We will go in to dinner now. Do not speak again to Mr. Alpert. It will displease me greatly! Come, my dear," and he smiled, as his mother came toward them.

"Are you keeping my daughter from me again?" she asked gaily, and slipped her arm into Caroline's. "Why, you are shivering, my dear! Is the champagne making you cold? Never mind, you shall have some coffee soon. I believe dinner is being served, dearest," she added to Rudi, and gave Caroline a comforting hug before releasing her.

Rudi took Caroline in to dinner. He seated her on his right, and his mother took her place opposite, with some gay words about how she would soon give up her place to the new countess.

She sat silently, except when prompted by a whisper from Rudi. He told her when to reply to the many toasts that were given, what to say, when to stand, when to be seated. She obeyed him like an automaton, fiercely resenting his power over her. She wondered why she obeyed him, but when his eyes rested on her face, when his hand touched her hand, or his voice murmured—she obeyed him.

She could see Greg from where she sat. He was silent, although Madame Zollner, who was seated next to him was chattering gaily to him. Caroline would catch some of her words, something about art and Austria and treasures. She was evidently trying hard to draw him into conversation and not succeeding. Greg was absorbed in his thoughts, and they were hard ones, from the white lines about his mouth and the look of suffering in his eyes.

Caroline forced herself to eat some of the meal. She wanted something to counteract the champagne in her empty stomach. Finally she felt better and was able to think a little.

Greg was considerably shocked at the news of her wedding. He had been stunned and worried. But the other guests were not. No, they were not even very surprised, except for Winifred, thought Caroline. Winifred was surprised, not pleasantly, and her face as she stared at the bride was not kind.

Perhaps Rudi had made promises to her, made love to her, thought Caroline, and felt a sudden pain at the thought.

Had Rudi made love to her, beautiful long-legged, blonde Winifred, who hung on his shoulder and adored him with her eyes? Probably. He was the kind of man who took what he wanted, and laughed at the consequences.

And protected his own, and defended his own, and hated his enemies . . .

Caroline started violently as Rudi touched her arm. "Yes?" she whispered.

"You have not answered me. What are you thinking, Caroline?"

She looked down at her plate, her mouth mutinous. She did not have to tell him her thoughts! He owned her body, he ruled her with an iron hand. But he could not rule her mind.

"You will tell me later," he said, with cold amusement. She shivered a little, and turned to her neighbor deliberately, to answer his remark.

And she knew fear. All these people gathered about the long festive table, with its Herrend china and shining glasses and heavy silver—all these were his friends, who would sit and nod if he told them calmly that he planned to murder his bride! All except Greg, who was in as much danger as she was.

If they did not save themselves, no one would save them. They were isolated in an ancient castle, near the border between Austria and Hungary. No one was near but the friends and servants of Rudi von Dornstein.

Someone down the table caught her eye, smiled happily, lifted his glass to her. "Happiness!" he called in English.

She stared at him. What a terrible mockery. She was in costume, playing a part she had not rehearsed. She was an actress, forced to fill in at the last minute, and she was in terror of her life!

Rudi leaned toward her. "Thank him!" he whispered.

She forced a smile to her lips. "Thank you," she said, not very clearly. The man nodded, smiled, drank, his eyes fixed on hers.

"Yes, you are very beautiful, my love," murmured Rudi's voice in her ear. "I was smart to hide you away for a week! At least I have had you to myself for a time!"

She caught Greg's glance. What was he planning? If only she could talk to him again. They might together be able to plan an escape.

But was there any escape from Dornstein Castle, or its tyrant owner? She did not know any. She was caught in the grip of a master charmer who mocked her even as he made love to her.

"Do not stare at Mr. Alpert so," whispered her tormenter. "I do not like it! You belong to me!"

She turned her blonde head slowly, her chin high. "I have told you," she murmured. "I do not belong to anyone! When this masquerade is over, I shall leave!"

"You shall never leave me," he said, quietly, his mouth suddenly set and grim. "Only death shall part us! Shall we drink to that?"

And as she stared at him, her eyes wide, he raised his glass, and smiled as he put it to his lips. His black eyes glittered with fury.

She clasped her hands together in her lap. Her hands were cold, very cold. She felt numb with fear. He meant it. Death. Only death would part them. When would it come? Soon?

Chapter 15

The dinner seemed endless to Caroline. She felt as though she had lived an eternity when finally all of them rose, and the countess led the ladies into another drawing room. Rudi escorted Caroline to the door, lifted her hand to his lips elaborately and kissed it before he handed her to his mother.

The gentlemen returned to the table, and their port and cigars. More champagne was brought.

The countess led Caroline to the other room, chatting gaily, though glancing at her keenly. She was not so blind that she could not see something was wrong, Caroline thought bitterly. But she would not help the girl she professed to love. Rudi was her life, her adored son, and she would do whatever he said.

Caroline sat down on a chair near the table where the countess was pouring out coffee. She did not enter the conversation, her mind was busy, busy, busy with the puzzle of Greg Alpert and Rudi von Dornstein.

Greg was scared of Rudi, and with cause. But what was the real reason behind the terror? His brother? The brother who had changed his name? Caroline sipped at her rich creamy coffee, paying little attention to it, or to the catty remarks of Winifred Hinteregger, who had paused near her, leaning over the back of a chair.

Casper. She suddenly remembered it. Neville Alpert had changed his name to Casper. He had been an army sergeant—World War II—Germany—they had talked about art treasures. It was coming back to her. As Greg and the other man had entered the darkened room where Caroline and the artist had waited, he had called the man Neville

She remembered now. It was an unusual name. Neville Alpert. Older than Greg, more sophisticated, with a strange look in his eyes, a knowing hard look, of cunning and toughness.

What was the truth? Caroline knew she loved Rudi, but she feared him also. What was he doing to Greg? What did he want from her and Greg? He had asked again and again about the art.

Greg had said that his brother feared the Nazis, but Rudi's family had fought the Nazis. That was fact. That was truth.

She sighed a little. Winifred's voice raised insistently.

"When were you married? When did the ceremony take place?" She bent closer to Caroline, and a strong whiff of her sensuous perfume struck Caroline's nostrils unpleasantly. She moved a little, slightly, to avoid it.

"Why—it—was" she answered slowly, then looked to the countess.

The countess supplied the date with a smile. "I think the days have run together for you, darling, on your honeymoon. Trust Rudi to find a refuge for himself and his bride even in the midst of a crowd. How like his father he is! I remember on our honeymoon, we went to my family's, and how crowded it was! But my dearest managed that we should be alone day after day." She smiled with delight at the memory.

"Caroline is not at all like the von Dornsteins," said Winifred, nastily. "That blonde hair, that pale complexion, and her American accent. Do you speak any German at all?"

"Very little," said Caroline quietly, defiantly, her mind coming back from Greg to the challenge at hand. She looked at the furious young woman and found a little pity for her. Rudi had probably promised her marriage, as soon as his mother came around to it. And now, to think that Rudi had married someone else—

But Rudi would probably soon reassure her that his "marriage" was a farce, and the "bride" would be gotten rid of—one way or another. By sending her back to America, or killing her.

But—but—

Caroline frowned again, her thoughts returning to the huge puzzle presented by the whole matter. Her brain felt clearer and sharper than it had for days. She had probably not received any drugs recently. If only she could think, think, and work it out. She felt as though the clues were in her hands, if only she could fit them together and make a pattern. This piece—so—and that piece—there—and then she could see the picture, and begin to understand—

"Met before?" Winifred's sharp voice was probing.

"Oh—in Vienna. We met in Vienna," said Caroline, quietly.

"Before then? In America? Rudi went to America last winter. Did you meet him in New York City?"

"No, I did not meet him then."

"It was very sudden," said the girl sulkily. Caroline wondered if she had ever been thwarted before in her life.

The countess allowed her gaze to rest for a moment on the long-limbed jet setter, and her eyes were revealing. There was amusement, contempt, some triumph in them, before she lowered them demurely to the coffeepot before her. "More coffee, Madam Zollner? A little cream?"

Did the countess think the marriage was real? Was Rudi deceiving her also? Caroline had a new puzzle before her. The countess seemed sincere in her affection. Had she too been tricked, for some devious purpose of Rudi's? Did he mean her to think the marriage was real, until some vague future day when he could tell her it was false, and that he meant to marry the gorgeous Winifred?

Caroline's attention was caught by a movement in the French doorway behind the countess. Just beyond the light, in the shade of the balcony, was Greg. He motioned to her urgently, then stepped back quietly. She lowered her head slowly in a nod of recognition.

Madame Zollner was holding the countess' attention. Winifred was speaking to another woman, something about clothes. Caroline stood up slowly, murmured, "I will get some air for a moment," and strolled quietly to the window.

She stepped outside, had her arm gripped tightly. Greg

whispered, "Caroline, promise me! You will say nothing more to him! Tell him nothing! Our lives are in your hands!"

"Greg, you must tell me. About your brother. Rudi and his family were not Nazis. Tell me what they have—what purpose—what evidence—about your brother—"

He glared down at her in the darkness. His grip tightened cruelly. "Evidence? Are you crazy?" he whispered, with a hiss. "They don't need evidence! They hate him! They have chased him for years! Von Dornstein was after him in New York last winter! He barely escaped. My God, he will kill my brother! Don't you understand—"

"No, I don't understand." She followed him as he pulled her deeper into the shade. "Greg, tell me the truth. What do they have against you and your brother? Why were we lured here? What do they want to know? What is it about the art treasures? Are they fakes? Are they stolen?"

She felt him shake with impatience—with rage—she had no idea what emotions were roaring through him. He stood silently for a moment, and she felt him calming, controlling himself.

"You must—must believe me, Caroline," he said, more quietly, in a whisper. "Believe me, they mean to kill us! They hate us all, you included! If you want to live, if you want me and my brother to live, you must help us. Don't tell him anything. We have to get out of here. I'll get you out of this castle if it's the last thing I do! We'll walk to Vienna, run, hide out—but we must get away!"

"But if you would tell me—only tell me—"

"No! They would torture you to find out! No, Caroline, it is best if you don't know." His voice dropped to a caressing murmur, he held both her arms tightly in his hands. "God, if I had only realized what danger I was putting you in, I should never have brought you. Forgive, me, darling. I didn't realize they would pull this. My brother tried to warn me how ruthless they were."

"Don't think of me," she said, urgently, more confused than ever. "Greg, listen, save yourself, get away! They can't do much to me. At least, I don't think they will—they have seemed kind at times . . ."

"You must not be fooled by them! They are clever devils, all of them! No, I'll get you away, my darling, I will get us both away. There has to be a way out . . ."

He pulled her close to him unexpectedly, and pressed

his mouth to her lips. She caught her breath in surprise, too amazed to struggle. He kissed her again, there in the darkness.

"I love you, Caroline," he whispered desperately. "We must get away! We will escape somehow . . ." And he kissed her again, a long kiss.

Abruptly, Caroline was yanked away from Greg. A familiar voice raged at them both.

"How dare you touch her. How dare you kiss my wife? My God, you try my patience—"

And Greg went staggering back from a hard right to his jaw. Rudi released Caroline to follow his enemy. As Greg reeled Rudi struck him again, knocking him to the ground.

"Get up, coward! Get up, fight like a man! Get up, or I'll kill you . . ."

"No, Greg, don't get up!" Caroline cried out, as Greg got up on his elbow, groggily. She caught Rudi's arm, as he was lunging forward. The steel under her fingers made her feel like a puny kitten. "No Rudi, Rudi, please—"

He glared down at Greg, who seemed indisposed to move. Caroline held her breath. Rudi spun around, caught her arm.

"All right, Caroline, come along. You seem not to understand the place of a Dornstein! You need discipline! Come, come with me—"

He was breathing so hard she could scarcely understand the words he flung at her in German. He rushed her into the hallway, and up the flower decorated stairway down which they had come in such state a few hours before.

He was rushing her along so fast, her feet dragged. He pulled her with him. He was saying cruelly in German, "He won't get far. I will find him—punish him—my God, I will kill him for the insult—to touch my wife—he dares—my God—"

A deadly fear was running through her as she was pulled along the long corridor. He opened the door of the suite, pulled her inside, his arm painfully tight on her arm. He drew her into the bedroom, dropped his hand.

"I will lock you in," he said, more coldly, precisely, in English. "I will lock you here, you will wait for me. I shall teach you what it means to obey your husband!"

He locked the door to the other rooms, then strode out and slammed the door after him, locking the door to the living room. Caroline was still trying to catch her breath as she heard him stomping out into the hallway, slamming the door after him, and locking it. She was thoroughly locked in this time—to await discipline!

"Discipline? What does he mean?" she whispered, her hands on her flushed cheeks. "Oh, God, will he kill me?" He had been in such a terrible rage. She had never witnessed such fury. His face had been white, his hands shaking with fury. And the way he had struck Greg!

What would the guests think if she did not return tonight? That was the least of her worries, she decided. Rudi would make up some plausible excuse, and they always believed him. She sank down into a chair.

The room was dim, only one lamp was on beside the bed. Trudi had laid out her nightgown and negligee on a chair. She would not return tonight, Caroline thought, bitterly. And even if Trudi were there, she would not dare go against her master's wishes.

What would he do to her? He was intensely possessive, even his mother could not come to Caroline without Rudi's permission. He was incredibly jealous and domineering. How he must have hated to see another man kissing the woman he had claimed for his own—with or without marriage!

And Greg's kisses, on her mouth. Caroline grimaced. They had been cold, hard, hateful, she realized. She had not liked them. They had tasted bitter, the ashes of despair, or fright.

Greg had kissed her a few times before. Light, almost brotherly kisses, not like these. Friendly affectionate kisses, and she had welcomed the warmth and interest he had showed.

Had she changed or had he? Or both of them? What had these Austrians with their hates and passions done to them?

She closed her eyes. Rudi had changed her, she thought. Whether she had wanted to or not, she had come to love him. She feared him—but she loved him also.

The truth. What is the truth?

The hardest thing in the world to find. The treasure without price.

What is the truth?

The words pounded around and around in her brain. She opened her eyes, found she was staring at her nightgown.

She might as well undress and be in bed when he came. He was quite capable of ripping off the splendid gown. If he meant to kill her, he might as well do it in bed, she thought, ironically.

And perhaps the sight of her in a nightgown might soften him. He did feel—some affection—toward her . . .

Slowly she began to undress, pausing to listen every few minutes for the sound of boots, the stormy sound of Rudi returning to punish her.

She removed the pearl necklace and earrings and the ring, and laid them on the dresser. She managed to unzip the back of the dress, and step out of it. She hung it carefully in the closet, where the bouffant white skirt billowed out. She stepped out of the white satin slippers, took off the white silk slip, and the dainty underclothes.

He dressed her like a princess, she thought sadly. Everything would soon be over. If she did not die, she would return to New York, to the plain, ordinary work she had known before.

With only memories—the memories of his kisses, his wild caresses, his arms about her, his whispers in English and German, the crazy things he said to her in bed, the way he held her tightly, the way he made love—

Only that left—

She put on her nightgown, and slipped into bed, leaving the light burning. Still he did not come.

It was another hour before he did. She was beginning to relax, even get sleepy. She stretched, yawned—then stiffened, for the door to Rudi's rooms was opening.

Rudi came in, looked down at her somberly. He wore his robe and slippers. His face was hard and unrevealing, his eyes flashing black. His jaw was tense.

Without a word, he removed his robe, and slipped into bed beside her. He bent over her, and began to kiss her wildly, moving his lips roughly over her chin, her mouth, her cheeks, her throat. She lay motionless, scarcely breathing, as his arms slipped about her and held her tightly.

But his hands were not cruel, they were gentle. Slowly she began to relax. He placed her arms about his neck. One hand slipped to the hem of her gown, moved it up. He bent over her and began to bring them together.

Was this his "discipline" and his punishment of her? What sweet punishment, she thought, in a daze, as his kisses burned through her, and his body moved over hers.

A groan built in her throat at the pleasure, she had to move to respond to him, and her arms tightened convulsively. She lifted herself up, and her long legs closed about his thighs.

He moved slowly, then faster, then moved swiftly to the climax, and brought her such keen pleasure that she cried out, gripping him, her eyes shut tight. She felt his pleasure come to him, and then they lay silently, clasped together tightly.

Finally he moved, to lie on his side, looking down at her. He pressed his hands lightly, lovingly to her breasts.

"Caroline," he said, in a controlled voice. "We must talk about this. I want to know. Do you love me?"

She opened her eyes slowly, looked up at him. Her mouth moved, but she would not speak. Rebellion was welling up in her.

"No, do not fight me," he said quietly. "Do not. I am in deadly earnest. This is a matter of life, of honor. Do you love me? Tell me the truth."

His hand pressed warningly on her, as her lips tightened. She closed her eyes. Would she say it? Could she? What was the truth?

Only the truth would do. She opened her eyes, looked up again at him. "I—love—you—Rudi," she said faintly.

His lips relaxed a little. He bent and kissed her cheek. "Yes, I know you do, my love, or you would not respond to me as you do. Only I had to hear the words from your mouth. Now, tell me, what do you believe of me?"

"Believe—of you?" she asked blankly. This was far from the cruel punishment, the fury and anger she had expected.

"Yes. Am I a man of honor? Or dishonor? A man who would cheat and lie and steal? Or what do you believe of me?"

"You are—I believe you value integrity above all things," she finally said, very slowly.

"Integrity, yes." He gave a little sigh. "Caroline, you must believe then that I act with—honor. That I am striving to right a wrong. That I will go without the law, but I will do what I believe just and right. Do you believe that?"

She did believe it. She nodded. "Yes, Rudi."

"Good. Then—you must tell me. Caroline, you must tell me everything you can remember about Greg Alpert, about his brother. What do you remember about the brother? You saw him in New York."

Greg had said they would capture him, torture him, kill him. Whom to believe? But she had already confessed she believed Rudi. She trusted him more than Greg, of whom she really knew little. She had to make a choice of loyalty, and make it now. She chose.

"His brother—I remember his name now. Neville Alpert. He changed his name to Neville Casper," she said, rather faintly.

He gave a little sigh. Of relief? Of weariness? Then he asked, "And what about the meeting in New York? Tell me again from the beginning. What did he say?"

She told him all she could remember. He prodded gently, and she remembered more details. He asked about a scar on the man's face, and then she recalled it, and described it.

Then his questions went to the work in New York, Greg's contacts. The artists who worked for him. He asked about a man named Jessup.

"Jessup? Oh, yes, one of the artists. I make out checks to him."

She felt Rudi stiffen. "Checks? How much?"

She told him what she could remember.

"Have you ever met him? Ever seen him?"

She frowned, thinking. "No—no, I never did. I never saw his art either. Greg said he was a fine artist, that his work sold to private patrons immediately. I told Greg I thought he ought to have a showing. But Greg did not answer—I thought at the time it was odd."

He asked for everything she could remember about Jessup, and she told him.

Rudi questioned her again and again. She was getting sleepy, and yawns interrupted her answers. She wanted to curl up in the big warm bed, and sleep, but his urgent voice kept interrupting.

"What about a man named Grimes? Have you heard the name?"

"Grimes. Oh—yes—he did engraving."

"What kind of engraving? How much money did he earn? Have you ever seen him? Where did you send the checks?"

They went on and on, until Caroline thought her brain would surely run dry. She was amazed at how much Rudi knew already, but he would not explain why he questioned or what the answers meant to him. He would interrupt her to ask another question, and his face blazed with eagerness and attention as she told him what she knew of Greg's work and contacts.

She thought he would never stop, but finally he did, and slipped her head down on his arm.

"There, now, sleep, Caroline. That is what I needed to know. Don't fret, darling, you have betrayed no one who deserved your loyalty. Tomorrow I think things will be revealed and explained. But we must wait and see."

"Where is Greg?" she asked, sleepily, nuzzling her head against her shoulder.

He hesitated, finally murmured. "Hush, now, go to sleep. You are weary, my love. Sleep," and he patted her cheek, and kissed her bare shoulder.

She went to sleep in his arms, feeling curiously at peace. She did not know if she had done right or wrong. She only knew that she had to be loyal to Rudi, when the chips were down.

She felt as though she were married to him, whether she truly was or not.

Chapter 16

When Caroline wakened, late the next morning, she was alone. But she knew that Rudi had remained with her all that night, she had felt him close to her, and they had been comfortable with each other as never before.

Rudi. She dreamed, smiling, still in a half-sleep, her mouth curving to the memory of his kisses. Finally, she stirred, yawned, sat up to get out of bed.

Trudi came in, smiled to see her, and went to the bathroom to draw her bath. Caroline asked for the blue dress with the white lace collar and cuffs—Rudi liked that one best, she thought.

She ate breakfast alone, slowly, not thinking very much, dreaming about the possibility of making a real marriage with Rudi, of living here with him. Was it true? Would it happen? She did not know. But what if—maybe—

Caroline felt restless. Rudi had said that today she would find out everything. She wanted him to return. She was locked in as before. She went to the window overlooking the gardens, but could see nothing special. Trudi had disappeared.

She went through her bedroom and Rudi's, to his study.

He was not there. She hesitated, then went to the garden door, and slowly walked down the winding stairs.

Dreamily she strolled down the cobbled paths, pausing to sniff a rose, thinking about Rudi, about last night, about the secrets he might tell her.

When someone grabbed her arm, she half-screamed in fright. A hand was clapped over her mouth.

Greg dragged her into the shade of a tree. "Hush! Caroline, it's me, Greg," he said roughly.

She stared at him, her heart racing. He was unshaven, mussed, his hair standing on end, a frantic look in his eyes.

"Greg! Where have you been?"

"I hid out all night. God, he is out to kill me! He had men chasing me all night. I finally got to his study, thought I could talk to you. But all your doors were locked."

She swallowed. "Yes—he—locked me in," she said faintly.

"Did he torture you?" Greg demanded, still holding her arm in a tight grip. He drew her with him deeper into the shadows, beyond the flower gardens.

She could not stop the betraying blush that strained her cheeks. Greg glared down at her as she did not answer.

"No, he doesn't have to use torture on women, does he?" he said roughly. "He charms them! What did he make you tell him?"

She was silent, remembering all she had said. Had she been charmed to betrayal? Was her judgment clear? Had she trusted the man deserving of trust, her husband Rudi?

Greg shook her arm cruelly. "What did you tell him? Did you talk about my brother?"

She faced him bravely. "Yes, I did, Greg. I—I remembered his name, Neville Alpert, only he had changed it to Casper."

He took both her shoulders in his hands and shook her like a child. "You told him that? My God. What else?"

"He—he asked questions. I—answered—oh, Greg, what is it? What have you been doing, you and your brother?"

"You little—cheat. You stupid female! I might have known you would queer it! Damn! Okay, I'll tell you. My brother got his hands on some art in World War II. He held on to it, sold it back to the owners with a pretty story, and plenty of money came out of it! But he ran out of the real stuff, and the game was getting hot. That was where I came in."

"Greg—oh, no—not stolen art," she whispered.

"Sure, baby. Sure." He was pulling her with him, deeper into the bushes, tearing her blue dress. She wanted to protest, he was deaf to her, yanking her brutally with him.

"Greg, don't—my arms—you are hurting me!"

"You betrayed me! Damn it. I didn't know you knew enough. Did he ask about anybody?"

She was silent, her mouth tight. She would tell him no more. She was frightened now, beginning to struggle against him.

"Well, you probably did," he muttered, half to himself. "God, you little bitch. Telling that Dornstein—and he was on to me. How I tripped up, I don't—but we got away with it for years. Slipped real art in with fakes, and nobody caught on to us, until Dornstein—and that Madame Zollner, clever bitch. I wish I had her on my side! But she was on to it. The real icon, and all that other fake stuff. She wasn't fooled, damn her!"

He was pulling her toward the cliffs. She tried to yank back, finally frightened and knowing what he meant. "Greg—don't—not the cliff—" she cried out.

"Yes, you devil! I'll get away, but I'll kill you first! Betray me? Others have paid high for that! Neville knew, he knows how to—answer people—who betray!" Greg was panting, dragging her bodily now toward the high edge of the cliffs that went into a sheer drop to the rocks below. She tried to dig in her high heels to hold them back. He picked her up bodily, and carried her closer.

"Greg, no. Listen—tell me how it worked, tell me—" She panted out anything, anything, to delay him.

"You know too much!"

"Last night—you tried—to get into my rooms. Why? To get me away—or kill me?"

He paused, glared down at her, his face that of a maniac. His mouth twisted in a cruel grin. "To kill you! I knew you would talk! You women—all too soft—I planned to kill you then!"

"I thought so," she said quietly. "Thank you, Greg. If I die, I will know I trusted the right man, Rudi von Dornstein! Thank you for that!" And she glared back at him in defiance.

"You can—think of that—as you—go down!" he yelled,

and pushed her and pulled her toward the cliff. She fought strongly, with all the energy of her young body, all the despair of a woman who wanted very much to live. She fought him back from the cliff, stumbling on the stony edge.

Then someone caught Greg from behind her, and lifted him high in his arms. It was the madman, Julius Mayer. His white hair was ruffled by the wind, his black eyes filled with hatred.

"Nazi! Nazi!" cried Julius, as he struggled with Greg.

The two men were locked in a terrible grip, but Greg still hung on to Caroline's arm in a frenzy of revenge. He glared at her even as he struggled to release himself from the madman.

"Greg—let me go—let me go!" she was yelling, pulling back from him.

"Nazi, Nazi," groaned Julius, pulling him toward the cliff, and Caroline was dragged along with the two men because Greg would not release her even to fight the other man.

"You'll—die—with me!" Greg bit out the words, in a frenzied way. "Bitch. Bitch! You—will—die!"

She tried to pull back. Julius was pulling Greg one way, she the other. Julius was yanking Greg toward the cliff, and Greg determined that she should go with them. She screamed, screamed again.

Two brown hands were in front of her, holding her firmly. Then one hand began striking again and again at Greg's upper arm as he held her.

Rudi. Rudi was holding her. With a sob, Caroline began to gather renewed strength. Rudi was there, she would not die. He would save her. She yanked hard, as Rudi struck again at Greg's arm, with the hard side of his hand in a karate chop.

Greg had to let go. His face twisted in a fury of hate, his eyes almost shut with the strain, but he let go, and turned to fight Julius.

But it was too late—too late for both of them. They were too near the edge of the rock-strewn cliff. Greg's foot slipped, he yelled as he went over, toppling over with Julius holding on to him in a mad death grip.

Caroline and Rudi stared down. The two doll-like figures finally separated in their slow almost floating drop into the air. Then—the rocks below.

Caroline shuddered convulsively as Rudi drew her back slowly, from the side of the cliff. "It is over," he murmured in German.

Caroline hid her face on his shoulder, and his hand went to her hair and held her tightly. She felt him shaking.

They stood there for a long while in the sunshine, shivering at the closeness of death. Caroline's knees began to buckle under her. Her arms hurt from the long struggle.

Rudi gathered her up in his arms, and began to carry her toward the castle. Kurt stood in the pathway, his scarred face convulsed.

Rudi spoke to him in German. "Take some men and horses, Kurt. Bring back the bodies. It is—over. He died—a hero, once more, our Julius."

Kurt nodded slowly, tears running down his cheeks. Rudi carried Caroline past him into the drawing room just off the gardens. He put her down on a couch. She lay there quietly, with her eyes shut, not sure she could ever move again.

She felt Rudi's hand stroke her hair slowly. "Caroline, ah, Caroline," he muttered, and put his face down against her shoulder. He too was near collapse, she thought. But her arms were too strained to reach out and hold him.

She lay limp as a rag doll—like those two figures—floating through the air to the rocks—crashing on the rocks. She shivered again convulsively, Rudi got up "You are growing cold," he murmured in German. She tried to move, could not.

She heard voices, the countess. "Julius—is he—my Julius—my brother," she cried, in a heart-broken voice.

"Yes, he died, a hero once more, Mother. I have sent Kurt for him. He—saved my—Caroline. Mad, he was more sane than—that other one."

The countess sobbed once, then said more strongly. "He died as he would have wished. I will go out and meet them. Is Caroline. . . ." And Caroline heard the rustle of her dress, smelled her delicate perfume as she bent anxiously over her.

She forced her eyes to open, she was able to smile feebly. "I am all right, Mother," she said, vaguely.

"Ah, my dearest," said the countess, bending over her, kissed her gently. "But she is cold, Rudi—she must have a blanket."

The needs of the living made the countess forget for a

moment her grief over the dead. She bustled about, brought coffee for the two of them, a blanket for Caroline, tucked her up, murmured and soothed her. Rudi was sitting on the floor behind the couch, his head bent, as spent as Caroline had ever seen him, exhaustion in the lines of his bronzed face.

She touched his head timidly, and he finally looked up into her face.

"I almost lost you, love," he said, finally in German. She realized he was so weary he could not bring himself to find the English words. She smiled down at him.

"We are safe now. Why was I so foolish—I could not see—understand—" she faltered.

"I should have trusted you, told you. I felt—felt you were good and fine. But I did not know how deeply involved you were," he said.

They said no more. But later when she had recovered somewhat she sat up, and declared, "Now I must know what was going on, Rudi. Please tell me something!"

The countess had gone out to attend to the sad duties of her dead brother.

Rudi sighed a little, brushed back his hair, and sat beside her on the couch. He took her hand in his, and played with it as he talked.

"I had begun to suspect several years ago, when I saw some treasures restored to some friends. Nothing big, just little details that puzzled me. I talked to Madame Zollner, she too had her suspicions. Then Greg Alpert brought some things to Baron Hans von Ehrenberg. Some were definitely authentic, which puzzled us. Others were—borderline. It is very hard to prove forgeries, my friends were fooled. How could I say to them, I believe these are fakes? I think you were deceived? Alpert put on a good appearance, he was too young to be involved in World War II."

"How did you guess, then?"

"The name Alpert. Some records turned up a sergeant in the American Army. He had been an art expert, and was involved in the restoration of stolen treasures. Yet some treasures were never found. Alpert disappeared. Years later, another man named Alpert, much younger, comes back with those treasures. And refuses to tell where they came from. I went to New York last winter, got a few leads, which always led back to Greg Alpert. Finally he contacted me, told me that he had the Dornstein Icon."

Her hands stirred in his, and he tightened his hold on them, and lifted one to his lips.

"Greg said—at the last," she told him quietly, "that the icon was real. It is the Dornstein icon. The rest are fakes and forgeries. He did say that."

"It is real? Thank you, darling. That relieves my mind. I can believe it now. I felt it was, yet the rest were dubious. Machines and chemicals could have proved something, yet I felt the icon was real. My only chance to learn the truth quickly, and capture Alpert in the act of trying to sell us stolen goods and fake goods, was to get the truth from you, which I did, darling. Thank you for your trust. I still don't know why you trusted me, instead of Greg."

Her voice faltered only a little. "Because—I love you, Rudi. I believed in you—your honor, your integrity. I had to make that choice. There was no other one to make."

He looked deeply into her eyes, then bent his head and pressed his lips to the back of her hand.

"Darling," he whispered.

"I want to know something," she gathered courage to say. She said it to his bent head, it was easier. "Was our marriage real or a fake? I was not—sure, Rudi."

He lifted his head, smiled, a little mischievously. "Didn't you know?" He pressed a kiss to her cheek. She turned her head away nervously. Was he going to tease her again, not tell her the truth?

"No, I don't know," she said, in a stifled voice.

He caught her up in his arms. "It was real, my love! It was very real, the best thing that ever happened to me. You see, I had fallen in love with you the moment I saw you, blowing down the street like a beautiful spring goddess! I knew at once I wanted to marry you. But I didn't know how much you were involved with Alpert's schemes. I felt you were innocent of any misdoing—and Mother swore by you, and swore at me!" He burst into a laugh, and she finally smiled with him.

"She—she knew about it all?"

"Yes, and was most reluctant to deceive you! She too loved you from the first, and trusted you thoroughly, with her sure feminine instinct. I should have listened to her, it might have saved you that—terror—by the cliffs!" His face hardened, his black eyes blazed once more. "When I think he almost killed you."

"He came up to the rooms last night, Rudi. If you had

not locked me in he would have reached me, killed me. He said so."

"My God!" he muttered, and his arms tightened almost painfully about her. "The chances I took—but at least I knew enough to guard my most precious treasure, you, my wife." And he bent and kissed her lips passionately and possessively.

She put her arms shyly about his neck, and gave him back kiss for kiss. She did not need to hide her emotions any longer. He loved her, and she was his wife, his true wife, forever.